ONE DAY
I WILL TELL YOU

First published in the United Kingdom 1990 by
PRION, an imprint of Multimedia Books Limited,
32–34 Gordon House Road, London NW5 1LP

British Library Cataloguing in Publication Data

Aburish, Saïd K.
    One day I will tell you
    I. Title
    813.54 [F]

ISBN 1 85375 067 0

Typeset by Wyvern Typesetting Limited, UK
Printed in the United Kingdom by The Bath Press

ONE DAY
I WILL TELL YOU

a novel by

SAÏD K. ABURISH

For Linda to earn her freedom.
And for my young friends Daniel and Oliver.

CHAPTER ONE

It was a little later than usual. The regular crowd had gone home. The odd hour and my manner told the publican that I had been drinking. He gave a smile of recognition which translated into "And what have you been up to?" But he didn't say it and instead introduced me to a tall, well-dressed blonde named Emma Johnson who looked very much the professional young lady who took her damned silly job seriously, in this case public relations.

She was as drunk as I was—and looking for action. The bastard behind the bar knew me better, but he was having fun and without any of the regulars to talk to, I decided to oblige and flirted with Emma, who more than returned the compliment.

By the time eleven o'clock came, Emma and I had already talked ourselves into an it's-too-early-to-stop state of mind. We decided to go to Annabel's to continue the party. The door staff at Annabel's were the same ones I remembered and they all said the same thing about it being a long time since they had seen me. Emma and I managed to wobble our way through the crowds in the hallway towards the dimly lit area where the bar was. Whatever friendly thoughts Emma had entertained about me were now enhanced by my familiarity with Annabel's.

Later good old Emma turned out to be a good dancer and my own traffic cop heavy steps were improved by drink, so we danced away while Emma made banal late-night confessions including the fact that it was her first time in the place. She told the disc jockey that Annabel's was really posh and asked him to play "Something" for her and then asked about all the people in black ties sitting in secluded corners. When we sat back at the bar, an American from the other side waved hello, which I answered, and Emma in a most natural way asked who he was.

Suddenly another world came back in full color, a world I thought I had put behind me. It took over as if Emma and all that public relations rot of the last three hours hadn't happened.

"That bastard is a spy, Emma. Look at him, so clean cut and innocent. Fucking hell, I wonder what he is doing here? Cape

Miller, fucking bastard would railroad his own mother." Emma made a mild objection to my language, but was more intrigued by why a spy would come to an open place like this. "Emma, I knew a spy in Beirut in the good old days who said a public place is the perfect spot for spies' meetings. He held court at the terrace of the infamous St. George Hotel, a few yards from where Kim Philby and Co. used to sit. Something which might interest you—spies are the smartest public relations people in the world. They keep everyone wanting to know more."

Emma was drinking very little now, but I was going full tilt. Eventually she asked how come I knew so much about spies and spying. I told her it was a hobby of mine and quickly asked her to dance again.

It was two in the morning. Emma held me close to keep me from assaulting other dancers who looked as if they didn't belong to the place, members of an office party, I had decided, occasional visitors who annoyed the hell out of the habitués. Something must be done about the bastards, I thought. The women were overdressed in an obvious, American high school prom way and the men's suits were badly cut. Fuck them . . . I knew what to do.

I remember the disc jockey tried to dissuade me, but I don't remember what he said. I got hold of the microphone which was plugged into the sound system and screamed at the top of my voice "Kneel and repent, the Lord is coming you sinners, kneel and repent. . . ."

Several hands were propping me up near the outside door and I vaguely remember a nervous, confused Emma telling them that I didn't have an overcoat and the head barman saying, "It's time to go home to bed, Mr. Daoud . . . that last bottle of champagne was a bad idea . . . it's time to go home. . . ."

Emma must have dropped me in front of my place and run away with the taxi. I don't remember how I made it up the stairs, but once near the top, as if in a dream, I heard a heavy landing of human feet on the patio and I listened and waited until I could feel myself sobering up as the feet sped away . . . yes, I am pretty sure they were feet.

Let's have it out . . . let's have it out you bastard, whoever you are. What the hell, I am going to go out swinging. There must be a broomstick somewhere . . . where is it? Oh shit, Mrs. Murphy, where the hell do you keep things? No, not in the bedroom, but there is a wooden coat hanger . . . I'll take this, walk down to the door of the patio and walk out. I'll surprise the bastard outside with this coat hanger. First, slowly now, undo the lock of the door, then careful don't fall down, kick the door and run out . . . yes, now.

"Emma, don't shoot until you see him clearly. Who the hell is there, who's there?"

Suddenly there was no Emma to frighten anyone, no gun, no intruder to be seen, just the eerie shadows of the empty London night and me on the patio with a wooden hanger in my hand challenging the whole wide world. Perhaps there had been someone. Perhaps he ran away . . . I just don't know. "Time to go home to bed, Mr. Daoud." Yes, it's time to go to bed. Tomorrow will be different. No, don't unplug the phone . . . they might call . . . they might have something to say this time.

CHAPTER TWO

I had written and rewritten the letter, and amended it four more times and was still unhappy with what it said. Time was slowly slipping away. I needed to post the letter. No, no . . . I didn't want to post the letter, but I wanted to have a response to what it contained. I really needed to meet her, Anna, and to talk to her. Emma Johnson, Cape Miller and remembering the Beirut days overcame the fears of the letter's contents with all its sloppy sentimentality, the open, unashamed and very painful cry for help.

Dear Anna,

The unusually cold June has given people the ready-made excuse to talk about the weather. This time the talk is justified and that makes it sound real. It is an acceptable reason for boring conversation. And though the whole thing is an excuse not to talk about other things, for me a strange relationship has developed between the bad weather and my present problems. The more depressing it becomes, the deeper I sink.

Also, people are full of gossip about Prince Charles and Lady Diana. You can't escape conversations about the weather and the Royals, stupid substitute conversations which hold no interest for me except to get me agitated and add to my uneasy state of mind which seems to have declared war on everything in sight.

So, I am writing after all these years because I feel a strong need to talk about something more real. This may surprise you, but I really want to talk about me, and even after all this time you come to mind first. You always said that one day I would tell you.

This is all a euphemism for a strong need to have a rap session, though I know talking about me isn't likely to be easy or make me happy and I may regret it. In the end I

*suspect I will feel empty and tired, but I still need some
relief regardless of what follows.*

*To hell with the weather and the Royals. Anna, I am
really tired. Call me please.*

Love,
Daoud

The wait for Anna's telephone call began the day after the posting,
accompanied by a sudden paralyzing recognition that it could be
another empty one, another reminder that they were still
monitoring me. I played mental games with myself, convincing
myself that Anna would ring at a certain hour, and was disappointed when it didn't happen. For minutes at a time I would look
at the telephone thinking my stares would induce Anna's friendly
call, but no such thing happened. I woke up in the middle of the
night, convinced I had heard a ring, and even picked up the
receiver only to be forced into rejoining reality by the sound of the
dialing tone. One time I even ran out of the bathroom dripping wet
to answer a ring or a call that was never there. Anna's telephone
call became the center of my life. But then why not? My daily
routine from the coffee shop to the pub had been the same for
months except for an increase in the level of drinking, usually after
they called. Reading didn't work. Concentration was lacking. I
would reread paragraphs dozens of times, but they stayed beyond
comprehension, after which I would resort to reading them out
loud to myself until I became hoarse. But they still didn't register. I
couldn't watch television because I couldn't see. My trembling
hands couldn't cope with inserting my contact lenses in my eyes
first thing in the morning, and when I did manage this delicate feat
the contact lenses wouldn't stay in because my eyes were dry.
Sleep took place an hour or so at a time. I usually came to when the
effects of alcohol wore off, but would sleep again when exhaustion
reasserted itself. Three days had gone by without any telephone
calls and the hope of a friendly response to the letter was fading.

The telephone rang early on the fourth day, just as I was ready to
start my daily coffee shop and then to the pub routine. For one
moment my heart stopped beating, but yes, it was Anna. Her voice
was the same as I remembered it, but mine cracked in spite of all
the mental rehearsals to avoid this.

"Daoud . . . hello. It's Anna."

"Yes . . . yes, I know."

"Listen, I just got your letter. I have moved since I saw you last. How are you? Things sound pretty bad!"

"I guess so. . . . It's a bit out of control."

"Daoud, come and see me. Come now. You were always an early riser and I'm not that far away."

I took her address and told her I'd be there in an hour.

I didn't want to rush, another fear of confirming the worst aspects of the letter. The confrontation I had asked for had become a painful prospect. So instead of hailing a cab immediately, I went to the Italian café to waste some time. I added *Time* magazine to my regular reading list, but my resistance didn't last long — the urge to go to see her asserted itself. I had one cup of coffee instead of the usual two and walked to Oxford Street where I got a cab right away.

My attempt to deal with the crossword puzzle in the taxi was a charade. I could hear my heart thump. I tried to think out all I wanted to say, but no thoughts materialized, not even the ones I had thought of before. I looked out of the window at a gray London, damp and sunless. Amazingly, I noticed things I had never noticed before; buildings, gardens, shops and the manner of people walking to work at that hour of the morning. It was as if a new extra sense had surfaced within me. I could feel a cold sweat developing on my forehead and I wiped it away with my handkerchief. I also had the strange feeling that the taxi driver looking in the rear view mirror recognized my condition to the point of almost talking to me about it.

Soon the taxi turned into the cobblestone road and stopped at number 30 which was in the middle, a mews house with a gray facade and a red door. The door opened as I was paying the taxi and Anna stood there waiting.

Our cheeks touched in politeness and very briefly. She hadn't changed, but direct looks were out of order. I noticed very little except my own shoes as I followed her up the stairs to the top floor. I silently moved along the steep narrow steps and the only sound was the swish of my feet on the thick carpet.

The room at the top had sliding glass doors on its eastern and western sides which made it light even on a dim day. The eastern side led to a small well-tended garden and the western side overlooked Metersham Place. The south wall was covered with paintings, most of which I remembered and didn't like. The other wall was one mass of bookshelves full of tomes about Africa and the Middle East, plus pictures of Anna in these places looking suntanned and very involved and happy with her surroundings. It was a good sized room done in good taste.

She asked me to sit down and I did, clasping my hands. Then she asked whether I wanted coffee or a Bloody Mary, making it plain that the occasion called for Bloody Marys. I agreed with a polite refrain about how early it was. The Bloody Mary came glistening red in a crystal jug and there were two large glasses which were placed on silver-covered coasters.

"Well, cheers," Anna said expectantly.

"Cheers—thanks for calling," I chimed in, hoping she would make the first move.

"You knew I would."

"Yes."

She didn't know what to say after that, so she asked about my parents. I told her that mother lived in Houston with my sister, having escaped Beirut about two years before. We made a little joke about her learning English at the age of sixty-two and that seemed to improve the atmosphere. Then we talked about my father and I told her that he was still in Beirut and still the same, and that all attempts to get him out had failed because, having left Jerusalem in 1948, he hated the idea of becoming a refugee for a second time. I spoke with some pride of the first rate reporting he had done out of war-torn Beirut for *Illustrated News* magazine. We both agreed that it was unbelievable for a self-educated man and we toasted him affectionately. Then we got carried away and toasted the Palestinians.

Anna continued to take refuge in conversation about my father. She asked me how old he was and when I told her he was sixty-four, she shook her head in amazement and said, "He is some fellow. I hear so much about him from other people."

"He is—sleeps very little, doesn't drink or smoke any more and works twelve hours a day."

"Do you hear from him?"

"Yes, I can't call Beirut from here, but he phones all the time, chats away, asks the same questions over and over again, the way they do at his age, really, and then he always ends up by telling me he worries about me a bit. Funny, someone in Beirut worried about someone in London."

Anna didn't laugh. "Why the worry?"

I took a heavy gulp of Bloody Mary, pretended to cough and with hand in front of face, opted out. "I'm not sure I know. He calls me more often than my brothers and sisters except Raouf, the youngest one. You remember Raouf, my youngest brother, the Sorbonne-educated PLO type. I guess it's nice in a way that he worries about me."

"I think a lot of people would worry about you—if you let them, but you never did. You've always got frightened when someone got close."

"That's an old conversation, Anna. I've never been interested in a lot of people. At this moment in time I don't care. Things have been a real mess. I don't know what to say."

"So you said in your letter. Hadn't you better tell me what it is? Why can't you come out with it?" The exasperation was beginning to show in her voice.

"Don't know why," I said. "Everything just fell ... fell apart. Nothing works anymore. Anna, I just don't know."

Her cheeks began to flush, became red on the spot. "For God's sake, don't do that—don't give me generalities. You always become vague, always so evasive, Daoud. Your letter was in Arabic. Alright, the language was English, but the manner was pure Arab. You always resort to this double-think. This ... you did it when you wrote the letter and you are doing it now. What are you trying to tell me? Why not let go for a change?"

She shook her head in despair and muttered something about going downstairs to mix more Bloody Marys. I stared out towards the west for a long time to take in all the Dickensian rooftops.

When Anna came back, I looked up, noticing her unmistakably long strides. There was a lot of bounce in her movements, though she had to be close to forty by now. She had kept her five foot ten inch figure in impeccable shape; the gray trousers and blue sweater suited her and she looked pretty. More Bloody Marys.

"Look, Daoud, what can I do if you are going to play your old game?"

"I'm not playing any game."

Our eyes met for the first time. There was a brief flash that recalled the most beautiful moments of our relationship. It was a rare instance of two-way emotional traffic which defied definition. Whatever it was that we once saw in each other was still there and I was shaken, and so was she. All of my pain was passed on to her and she accepted it and pleaded with me to speak. Christ, speak about what? I can't get her involved. I mustn't. It's too damn dangerous. The letter did say I wanted to speak, but really I didn't want to. I really didn't want to—I can't. I just wanted to be there. I was safe there. I was with a friend and I wasn't alone. Jesus Christ Almighty, I wasn't alone. The moments of terror induced by the empty telephone calls which spoke a language of fear I alone understood were far away.

She recovered first. Her voice changed and it was slower than usual, calmer, and she wanted to know what I had been doing and looked pained when I said nothing except drinking. The drinking was getting worse and perhaps my father had heard about it. Perhaps that's why he worried and telephoned as often as he did.

There was another uneasy lull in the conversation and Anna looked away while telling me that she had kept up with my news through our mutual friend, Felicity, and that Felicity had told her about my plans to go to the South of France to write a book about my family, a microcosm of social change in the Middle East. She said she had been happy to hear that, pleased for me to be doing something that I should have done a long time ago. Then she inquired about what had happened to the South of France and why the project never got started, and when I answered her with a cliché that "The road to hell is full of good intentions", she snapped back, "Daoud, are you going to play games with me all day long or are you going to tell me what's up? Hey you, it's Anna. You started this thing, remember? Cut out the bullshit, tell me what's up." She kicked the small table lightly in a gesture of make-believe.

"I will, in a while. Give me time. Writing a letter is easy, but face to face, Christ." I shook my head in despair. "I'm really not as tough as I look. So please . . . a bit of patience. Give your old friend a little time."

She moved and sat on her knees right in front of me and she took my right hand and put it between hers. Then suddenly she put my hand aside and let her head rest on my knees and she shook it right and left without lifting it. She raised her right hand without looking at me and moved it around my side and then upwards to the top of my shoulder which she gripped and squeezed gently. If I hadn't known her and wasn't accustomed to her voice, it would have been impossible to decipher her words.

"I know you aren't tough, you jerk, believe me I know. I'm not the one who made that mistake, you made that mistake. You made it, you're the one who pretended to be tough. You're the one who made-believe all the time. Thrashing away, you know, on and on, something inside pushing you, something inside keeping you away from everyone who got near. No, Jesus, no you aren't tough, you aren't tough at all. You are the loneliest man I ever knew and that's not new. That's been there all the time. You made it so difficult for others. It had to catch up with you and it did. Well, well!"

I lifted her head and looked into her eyes. I kissed her forehead three or four times before she backed away to her chair. "I'm not disturbing the peace am I? Is there someone who'd resent my presence here?"

"Not to worry. They come and go. They get younger and sillier. They're told from day one not to get heavy, but they still do. No there is no one."

"I am sorry."

"Don't be, it's my decision. It's my life. I see more of the girls now than I do men. I don't have big problems. I don't reach, darling, I'm not out to conquer. What the hell happened to bring it to this, you proud bum? In spite of the double-think, it took a lot to write the letter. Pride and pretense didn't stop you—that's not you. Something serious has gone wrong." She continued to shake her head.

"To hell with the pretense Anna, I really don't care anymore. Let's say that's true."

"What has gone wrong and why don't you care? If you don't care, then why are you here? Are you in danger?"

"I don't know. I honestly don't." And not knowing what else to say, I took the easiest way out. "Are there any more Bloody Marys?"

She nodded a bit unhappily, I thought, towards the stairs.

I ran downstairs and came back with the third pitcher of Bloody Marys which was waiting in the kitchen.

"Christ, I haven't done this in ages. It's ten in the morning and I'm already loaded. I don't drink early. I never drink before eleven, I promise."

"I'll get you something to eat. When was the last time you ate something?"

"Yesterday noon. I just forget nowadays. I don't get hungry and I forget to eat. What the hell, I lose weight and I look better don't you think?" I tried to giggle, but it didn't work.

"You look like hell. The bags under your eyes are a mile long, your face is puffy and the twinkle in your eyes is all gone. What is it, money? Or is it her? Surely not money. You could always manage money. So it's something else — something serious. It's her isn't it, you finally fell in love?"

I thought I would die. I certainly wanted to. My condition was more obvious to her because she hadn't seen me for a while, but the bit about the twinkle in my eyes hurt because years ago she had let go enough during lovemaking to make me promise never to lose the naughty laughter in my eyes. God Anna, I thought silently, that's really cruel.

"Well, one thing I know is that I'm hungry — and you must be. Fix yourself another drink. There are things in the small fridge around the corner on the landing. I'll go downstairs and make a cheese sandwich or something."

Anna didn't want to take back what she had said and I took refuge in another drink, a vodka and soda this time. Alcohol was finally producing the usual effect. It reduced fear, aches were forgotten and unsolved problems found ready answers. I was feeling better, a hell of a lot better, because of the drinks and the way things were going.

My part of the conversation had been about nothing, about the unknown, but then that's safe. I wanted to keep it that way, in spite of Anna's protests, to avoid having any regrets later. Christ, if only I could keep it this way and meet with her again and again and again. Hell, that's too much to ask of anyone. She has her life to live. It's generous of her to do this, but then I would have done the same for her. Come to think of it, I wouldn't have. I was always intolerant of others' weaknesses. Now I had mine to cope with. Many people would love it — me on my knees. But I am not really down am I? The hell I'm not. If I'm not in a bad way, then why the sudden reverence for my friends Maria Clark and Andrew, the suicides in my life? Perhaps I could do it by accident or half design, booze and sleeping pills. Perhaps that way, but not with certainty. It's the prospect of pain which frightens me, not the going. No! It's the going. It sure as hell is the going. I really don't want to go.

The result is a desire to curl up into a donut and kick and cry and clutch my stomach and wail. Something had to be released. How to do it? How to relieve what's inside—stop the sinking in a dignified way? This huge human heave, this cry of agony, of painful assessment. The last rites. Yes, the last rites and in that case they had to be done right. They should have a measure of dignity to them. Dignity must be maintained, even if the way out is alien to my nature, even if it is suicide.

If only I could do it—reach into the rusty recesses of my mind and talk to her, tell her. What a fraudulent thing to do, to ask to talk to her and then opt out. Come on, it is cowardly. That's what it is, cowardly.

"Here we are. Ham and cheese and most of a bottle of white wine."

"Looks good."

The tray was placed on the coffee table. Silence while we rehearsed our next round. Would she have a way of releasing me from my promise to talk? I couldn't think of an excuse. I was happy munching away at my sandwich and gulping the wine. Why say anything except what the situation demanded? It couldn't be helped, it had to be me. After all, I had started this confession.

"Do you feel better?"

"Much better."

"What are you going to do now? I'm off to deliver some picture frames. That's what I do for a living: frame pictures. I've got a complete workshop in the garage. That and the money my uncle left me do the job."

"Is the money department alright? I could. . . ."

"Don't, just don't. You men are good at offers like that. Everything except what matters." She criss-crossed her hands quickly in front of her face in a gesture of finality.

"That's not fair."

"Yes, it is, and deserved. Every time a man does the wrong thing he gives his woman a present. He tries to buy her back. Anyway, what you are going to do?"

"Go back home. You've never been there. You should. . . . Big enough for an office and flat above. A woman would do wonders with it, but she took her few things away."

16

"At long last. You wouldn't talk about her before, would you. Do you want to tell me now?"

"No."

"Why not—isn't that it? Isn't she the cause of all this?"

"No. She left because of me, not the other way around. I am the problem."

"We're back to Arab nonsense. You're so annoyingly pompous sometimes. . . . Listen, I must go. Will you call me? I'm in the book."

"No, but I will write another letter. Writing letters is easy."

"A letter from South Audley Street, from around the corner?"

"Yes, it's easier."

"It's silly. Plain stupid, that's what it is."

"It is easier." I stopped myself from saying "and much safer".

I remember springing to my feet and thanking her with a big, heavy hug. I remember shivering, then leaving without looking at her. I remember running down the stairs and out on to the cobblestone road which exaggerated my clip clops with its echo, then I turned right out of the archway and hailed a cab to Montpelier Street, my regular pub, for a few more drinks. It was about 11:30. I remember Anna and I had spent two and a half hours together.

Anna, Anna. . . . The only one among them who remained a friend and the only one where parting didn't hurt either side. Somewhere along the way, we had started becoming friends and as that grew interest in sex diminished and eventually disappeared.

Africa and the Middle East had given her a different outlook which allowed her to grasp notions and know people. Her intellect and emotions were in balance. There was also elegance and a legendary loyalty to friends—what lay behind the letter. Years ago, we kept each other friendly company without expectations for six months. I actually saw her every once in a while after our affair ended only I stopped seeing her when Maggie appeared on the scene because Maggie was jealous and I was in love and didn't want problems.

A taxi back to South Audley Street. I made it up the steep stairs past the first floor and on up to the top floor where my cat always waited for me. I petted the animal perfunctorily, went into the kitchen and took some ice cubes out of the freezer. A very large vodka went on top of them. For a moment, I held the drink with one hand and, behaving as if I was defying the inner voices that said don't do it, I gulped half of it down.

I ran downstairs to the lower floor, to the place I had used as an office, looking for paper and a pen. I wanted to sit down and write a letter to Anna. The more I looked at the paper, the more distinctly visible she became. Then I gulped down the second half of the drink. The effect of this on top of the Bloody Marys and wine did the job. Even for me, it was too much and I was fading. I was in no condition to write anything.

I went back upstairs to the kitchen which I didn't like. I placed the rest of the ice cubes in a deep glass bowl, took them with my empty glass and a bottle of vodka to the bedroom and tried to go to bed, though I knew I couldn't fall asleep. I wanted to be in bed because sooner or later Ecstasy would come in, jump on it and sit next to me. Perhaps she would even purr. Any friendly sound would be welcome.

The curtains were drawn, the noise from Park Lane was thudding and distant, the bedroom was dark and there I was pouring myself vodkas on ice and drinking them away fast, trying to induce sleep. Instead there were the images of what I wanted to tell Anna or what I would write or tell her if I could. There were shapes to the things I really wanted to say. They became very clear during these moments between total drunkenness and sleep. That is when they were real. That is when neither ego nor the wish to absolve oneself or lie mattered. That is when the past haunted me.

CHAPTER THREE

When the telephone rang at 7:00 p.m., I was in a semi-restful trance staring at the barely visible ceiling in a contemplative Arab way without anything specific in mind. I picked it up to listen to the live wire, fully aware that whoever was at the other end was listening attentively but unlikely to speak. Having expected the call, I was totally determined not to lose my temper and shout at them. "Please stop this," I pleaded. "Who are you and what do you want? You've done this for over a month now. Either tell me what you want, or stop it. I'll give you ten seconds." I didn't expect an answer and none came. I hung up knowing that as in the past they wouldn't call again.

I walked to the curtains, parted them and looked at the five story modern building across the street. There were lights in the windows, but no sign of life. It was a silly, instinctive exercise; they weren't watching me, they were doing something else. Who knows?

I resumed my empty staring at the ceiling, more awake than before, thinking about Anna's question as to what happened. She should ask THEM, I thought, the wonderful folk who gave us the Gulf War, the use of fourteen year olds as cannon fodder and chemical warfare, because one of them, perhaps more, had just telephoned. But if I had told her about the telephone calls, she would have become apprehensive; then there would have been no Anna and no one to spar with and I needed her. So selfishness prevailed. Still, the caller or callers were forcing me into another round of thinking about what happened and how it all began.

Well Anna, the problem started ages ago with Radio Freedom, the anti-communist organization with the pompous, ridiculous name. It was right after Princeton in 1968. The only thing I knew about Radio Freedom was television ads showing a supposedly Eastern European kid with black eyes looking from across barbed wire towards freedom, the West, and that haunting, faraway look towards freedom stayed with me and everyone who saw the ads. Remember things were different then; it was the year of the

Prague Spring and the invasion of Czechoslovakia and Radio Freedom was supposed to reflect American unhappiness and tell Eastern Europeans the truth. I never suspected for a moment that my association with that kid with the big black eyes would lead to this.

Because most people leaving universities were drafted and proceeded to do their military service, there wasn't any sense in looking for a job. After the right university and fulfilling the call to duty, the big corporations smiled and offered good positions. That's what I wanted to do and that is when I ran into Michael Wilson, on, of all places in the world, the corner of Forty Second Street and Fifth Avenue.

Michael Wilson had been a friend of my father fifteen years before; he had reported for the *New York Chronicle* from the Middle East. I recognized him in the middle of the location's usual pushy crowd and rushed through dozens of New Yorkers to tap him on the shoulder and introduce my new self. People his age change very little while I, at twenty-two, had no resemblance to the Arab kid of eight he had known.

He was visibly glad to see me. He gave me a card and asked me to come to see him at Radio Freedom the following day. He made it very clear it wasn't the usual perfunctory invitation and that he really wanted to talk to me. There was an unusual kind of insistence. He said that he wanted to show me the offices of Radio Freedom the following day and "buy me lunch". I enjoyed his obvious interest and accepted it as a compliment.

The next day I went to see Wilson at Radio Freedom's news offices. During our conversation I gave Wilson a brief, naive assessment of the Middle East: Nasser was a good man and the traditional people were bad. Also I, as a Palestinian, loved Nasser because he was trying to recover my country. My idealistic monologue continued as we walked from Wilson's unimposing office to a small Italian restaurant.

Wilson nodded with politeness and at the end of the lunch he asked me whether I would consider working for Radio Freedom in lieu of going into the army, after mumbling something about the world being more complicated. He described the offer as, "Eight hundred dollars a month, an expense account and a posting to Beirut." My job would be to listen to Arabic language broadcasts emanating from East Berlin, Moscow and Tirana, Albania, analyze their language and contents and help with preparing answers. More intriguing, I was also supposed to consider the possibility that the broadcasts carried coded messages. The Americans showed little concern for who listened to such broadcasts and whether they believed them; telling the Russians off mattered more.

Wilson never asked the obvious question of why wasn't I returning to the Middle East, but a year later, with deliberateness, he told me that he had decided that being American was more comfortable and pleasing to a displaced Palestinian than returning to a refugee status in other Arab countries. We both implicitly accepted my commitment to America.

Radio Freedom seemed like a fun job, certainly much better than being a simple soldier in the US Army. I readily accepted, without asking a single question.

That's how it all started, Anna. The first step in the trip to nowhere.

I wasn't in a hurry to start working, but Radio Freedom was. Loads of forms had to be filled out and they covered everything from my birthmarks to my parents' allergies and mercifully included some more serious stuff like my ability to think in two languages, communicate clearly in at least one and my belief in Radio Freedom, the US and God, in that order. The possibility that my other side, my Arabism, might create conflicts didn't occur to me or to Radio Freedom.

Two weeks of education and indoctrination followed. It was obvious that Radio Freedom and the US Government were related, if not one and the same, but I didn't expect this to matter. I was too far down the ladder, though I could tell after a while that I was a natural recruit. I had the appropriate background for the job and, through my father, the right contacts—the result of thirty years of Middle East reporting.

My indoctrination program was made easy by the type of people involved, the Eastern Establishment lot with a heavy tilt towards Ivy League colleges. They knew all about me, liked me and were full of offers of help and cooperation. By the time the intensive immersion in Radio Freedom's ways was over, buzz words were being used to describe me: "Our man in Beirut", "Our Middle East analyst".

Soon I was sent to Beirut and briefly devoted my time to

organizing myself in a two room, functionally decorated flat where I lived and worked. Then followed the basics of registering with the Press Association and meeting press attachés and government spokesmen. I also established my presence with the desk of the St. George Hotel, the center for the press corps, as a place to receive mail, cablegrams and other messages. There were no telex machines then and my pompous cable address was "Freedom Man".

All of these logistical necessities were placed against a background of pseudo-westernization which had overtaken the once attractive seaport. The clash of colors and temperament between East and West showed itself in everything from how people dressed and hailed a cab to how they endured the sound of the muezzin while in a sophisticated multilingual bar.

The pace was pleasant: two or three hours in the morning listening to newscasts, reading local newspapers and magazines, followed by a working lunch at the St. George Hotel or thereabouts which inevitably produced the oddity of British and American spies propping up one of the local bars. After that usually came a siesta, followed with an hour or two of writing my analyses of what the communists and the locals were saying, what I had heard and read. In between all of that, and not subject to routine, were the meetings, interviews, telephone calls, and the occasional two or three day absences from the tedium of monitoring broadcasts — trips to Amman, Damascus, Baghdad and other Middle East capitals to write special background reports.

Of course there were my undemanding parents, though at times they gave the impression that they suffered from a hurtful neglect. My father was a St. George Hotel regular, knew everyone and introduced me to dozens of people. He didn't worry about me then, though we often discussed news stories in an easy, relaxed way, and he dropped the occasional hint as to how to do it. My mother telephoned on a fairly regular basis to invite me to lunch or dinner which meant a sumptuous Arab meal plus an update on the performance of my brothers and sisters, all of whom were away at boarding schools. Whether, like all parents, they wondered about my personal life was something I never discovered.

Six months after arriving there, signs began to appear that Radio Freedom was half my job, the front half of it. The hidden, more important half, consisted of helping certain people in gathering military and other information of an extremely sensitive nature, particularly about the then leftist regimes in Syria and Egypt and equally important material on the political stability of the government of King Hussein of Jordan.

A brief, routine visit to Radio Freedom's news headquarters in Munich produced a perfunctory confirmation of the covert assignment. I was told to de-emphasize the listening post business and concentrate more and more on the second activity. My instructions were to come from the head of Radio Freedom's regional listening post in Athens. However, for the immediate future, my lead contact was in Beirut, a person already known to me albeit superficially: Jimmy Darrells, a tall, sophisticated American graduate of Yale, known for his love of long cigars, handsome Lebanese youngsters and Brooks Brothers clothes. Darrells pretended he was a wheeler-dealer representing American companies trying to secure work in the Middle East. He was, among other things, a consultant to Dage Communications, a leading defense contractor specializing in military electronics, a corporation with a wink-wink secret relationship with the US Government.

Darrells came to the St. George Hotel to see me, said nothing about what type of help he might need and appeared to want to know more about me as a person than about how I could help him. Unlike the polite Radio Freedom boys in New York, he was blunt. He had grown up on a farm in central Illinois and neither Yale nor Brooks Brothers was enough to cover the built-in midwest straightforwardness. He made an approving comment about my clothes, dropped a hint against spending too much time at the St. George Bar, asked whether I had a girlfriend and was pleased to note that drink made me quiet rather than otherwise.

Darrells' first call for help was to determine whether the Syrians had enough electric power plants installed around their northern port of Latakia to operate submarine pens. It was obvious the United States Government was concerned about Syria's willingness to grant the Russians port facilities which would allow their submarines to operate freely in the eastern Mediterranean.

Beirut was teeming with Syrian exiles, people who opposed the socialist government. They were capitalist, pro-West and ready to help. Though most of them couldn't have kept a secret if their lives depended upon it, an American call for help would enhance their status with other exiles. The information we needed was probably available, but the problem remained—who to ask without spilling the beans? I asked a St. George Hotel waiter, who often voluntarily whispered things in my ear, to tell me the name of a knowledgeable Syrian, and he gave me the name of the owner of a restaurant two blocks away. The restaurateur, rightly assuming I was working against Russia, freely told me all. In a matter of three days, he gave us detailed information about the capacity and location of all power generating plants in question. There wasn't enough power to operate the suspected submarine pens. American fears were unjustified.

Remarkable how the details of the beginning came back to me with ever increasing clarity when I drank too much and got one of my telephone calls, or was it the other way around? I remembered something new every time, but I still kept repeating the journey, looking for something that I still didn't have, a single clue as to where it got out of hand.

One time walking down South Audley Street absent-mindedly, I bumped into someone on the pavement, apologized and kept walking with a grin on my face because for a very brief moment I wanted to ask the rather pleasant looking man to tell me whether he thought spies were bad people or just ordinary people caught up in a dirty business which governments sponsor and perpetuate in the name of vague ideology. What fun it would have been to watch his face, to see him examine me from head to toe and say "So this is what spies look like—dizzy and dishevelled and so inept they can't walk down the street without bumping into other people. You don't even look like Philby, young man."

Yes, Anna. . . . What happened to bring it to this?

Enough mental search. It was about 8:00 p.m. and I had to decide what to do, to stay home or to go to a place full of human noise where I could be alone. It is ghastly outside, I thought, and I am tired, so perhaps I'll stay home and try to tackle the stack of magazines I have had for a week without reading. First more ice to make the first vodka palatable, then the BBC World Service which, though in German at this hour and I don't understand German, provides a needed assurance that I am in contact with humanity, and on to sleep, that most elusive of commodities. Alone into the night, counting the hours with no expectations or hope, organizing to waste another night, another bit of life lost to doubt and fear laced with enough alcohol to make doubt and fear faintly bearable.

Enough of this. I wish I could understand German. They just mentioned Arafat's name. I wonder what he has done this time? God, now Khomeini and Saddam Hussein. . . . Well I will wake up later and listen to it in English. I want to know what they are up to. What the hell is Khomeini up to this time? This is the only way to listen to Khomeini's news, in bed with a vodka in one's hand. . . . Yes, I wish one of the magazines was a girlie. . . . Ha ha, that would really complete the picture. Hell, I can't take this anymore, I'll go to the pub now.

CHAPTER FOUR

I don't remember whether it was the first or second week of April, 1969 when this particular meeting with Darrells took place, but I distinctly remember a change in his manner as he sat on the St. George Hotel terrace, right on the water. Even the old pro in him couldn't muster the phony grin, his second nature. He was bothered enough to forego his usual inquiries about the waiter's health and family. He went directly into hard conversation without the agonizing build up he usually went through while you prayed that he would get to the point.

"Daoud, we have a problem. We need someone good in Zahle to monitor the flow of arms from Syria to Moslem elements here. Syria is trying to start something. The arms traffic is likely to get heavier and Zahle is the natural gateway." Every word came through as if in a television commercial, with the right degree of middle class emphasis.

"God, Jimmy, I wouldn't know how to go about that. It's got to be a Zahle resident, someone who can get around and talk to people without difficulty. I just don't know," I pleaded.

"What about the Armenian guy, the one who wants to represent Zahle in Parliament?"

"You mean Sarkisian, the Newsreel cameraman, von Reibitz's assistant? He's usually with the reporters who gather inside, in the bar." I was too shocked to respond normally.

"Yes. You told me two weeks ago he is thinking of running for Parliament. Does he live there?"

"Yes, he does, but I told it to you as a joke. Even a joker in this country wants to be a member of Parliament. He doesn't stand a chance. He's happy being von Reibitz's leg man."

"Didn't he sort of ask you to speak to the Americans to help him win a seat in Parliament?"

My God, he's already made up his mind. "Yes, but the guy is simple, he's—"

"Never mind all that. He lives in Zahle and that's what we need. Can I meet him? I'll talk to him." Now he was resorting to the tactic of issuing orders.

"Directly? Isn't that going rather too far?"

"You just gave me the key word. If he's simple, then he is our man. Get hold of him and we will meet here in two days—same place at six. Call me. If he's coming, then William Saroyan is writing and if he isn't then he's got writing cramps. I must be off to see this little shrimp running for President. His Excellency is the most haughty beggar I've ever met. Must go." Darrells walked off without offering to pay for the drinks.

Sarkisian was very easy to find because he came to the St. George every day at eleven in the morning looking for von Reibitz. The following day, I invited him for a cup of coffee only to find him more depressed and depressing than usual. Newsreel International had fired von Reibitz two days before for drinking reasons, leaving poor Sarkisian uncertain about his own future and lamenting the drunken German's fate.

I told Sarkisian an American friend of mine wanted to see him to discuss his possible candidacy for Parliament which cheered him up, producing a wide grin which revealed a gold capped tooth I hadn't seen before. To poor Sarkisian, meeting with an important American gave him an instant uplift which made him forget about his more immediate problems; it was better than job security. Darrells was delighted to hear good old Bill Saroyan was productive again.

Sarkisian and I arrived first and exchanged lengthy Middle East banalities. Darrells arrived a polite few minutes late wearing a broad smile, slightly broader than usual. He stepped on to the terrace from the bar taking long certain steps and got to us in six or seven easy strides, stretching a firm hand to Sarkisian.

"Jim Darrells, I am very pleased to meet you, Mr. Sarkisian."

"Baron Sarkis Sarkisian. I am pleased to meet you too, Mr. Darrells." Sarkisian nodded.

I couldn't help it. Much to Darrells' dismay and Sarkisian's embarrassment, I giggled.

"Sarkis, I didn't know you were a Baron. When did this happen?"

"My father, Allah bless his soul, was made a Baron by the Sultan of Turkey. It's a hereditary title." And with that he gave Darrells his card, title and all.

Darrells took the card without a word and then proceeded to quiz Sarkisian on his life and family. It was a study in contrast, little five foot five Sarkisian with his old-fashioned double breasted suit, neatly swept back brown hair, hawk nose and trimmed mustache speaking preciously, desperately trying to muster up all the old world charm at his command, and Darrells tall, bespectacled his hair crew cut businessman style, being totally assuming, patronizing, his every act establishing him as master and reducing Sarkisian further and further. Darrells was in his element; he loved every moment of it. I didn't know whether the poor Armenian had been kicked about so much he no longer cared, or whether it was part of his larger refugee make-up which make people like him oblivious to insults.

Darrells told Sarkisian what he wanted and the latter was nodding agreement so hard I thought his head would fall off. The Armenian's only comment was a request to help him send his kids to an American university and Darrells answered that it could be arranged. In half an hour, Darrells left me with an ecstatic Sarkisian who summed up the situation with, "The Americans are a great people. When do I get money?" I promised to get him some money the following day and he left taking abnormally long steps. I had the feeling that he thought that is the way Americans walked, though he looked utterly ridiculous with his beak in front of him, hopping like a sparrow.

Darrells gave me two thousand dollars to give the Armenian, allowing as to how it was too much, but that Sarkisian would go to work right away thinking more was on the way. He also told me that *Al Sattar*, a loud daily newspaper, would soon run a pro-Sarkisian story. I made a mental note to look for it because the newspaper boys seldom had any and most copies went to the US Embassy, and some eventually to Washington to reassure the powers that be of the existence of pro-US newspapers in Lebanon.

Sarkisian's reports were accurate. Not only was he in a good geographic position to use his handful of local followers to monitor arms traffic through Zahle, but he had useful contacts with Armenian officers inside the Syrian Army, another case of ethnic bonds transcending national identity. His story was consistent: the arms were being smuggled into Lebanon, but they were light arms and didn't pose the threat imagined by the US.

The ethnic monitoring operation headed by Baron Sarkisian came to a sudden end after three months in circumstances which I never fully understood. Sarkisian had telephoned from Zahle and requested that I go there to see him as a matter of urgency. Darrells was away in Washington and going to Zahle was against the unwritten rules, but Sarkisian was in trouble.

"Please, you must come to see me. There is trouble, Mr. Daoud. You are my friend, I depend on you. Tomorrow, I will be in the big café on the River Yasmine. Please my friend, I am so sorry, but we talk tomorrow."

I had used the only taxi driver I could trust, Abdel Karim, and asked him to take me to Zahle and Yasmine. Abdel had grinned and winked and then suggested that I must be in love because only people in love made the twenty mile trip to the resort to meet a girl. What a good idea, Abdel Karim, I had thought. Then, to support his suspicion, I had asked him to drop me a hundred yards before reaching Yasmine and volunteered to walk the rest of the way because the lady in question didn't want to be seen . . . wink, wink. We reached Zahle in late morning.

Yasmine was oddly empty from a distance, but I had never been there before. A policeman materialized in front of me asking questions. This dictated that I continue towards the café. Turning back would have been too suspicious.

"You can't enter, sir. There has been an accident."

I produced my press card. He read it agonizingly slowly, then he looked at me and told me that the local Armenian candidate for Parliament had been attacked by a young man with a knife and killed.

"Probably another Armenian. After all, they're always feuding." I heard all this as we moved slowly towards the middle of the open air café.

Poor Sarkisian, on a cement floor, eyes open and neck and chest covered with blood. He looked as if he had been doing what came naturally to him: pleading. No, no I shouldn't touch him. Christ, I am about to be sick. Some water please. No, no not to drink, to splash on my face. Just an hour ago, a young man ran away, but there are three witnesses. It was too early for people to be there. No, foreign correspondents don't get accustomed to the sight of blood. Of course I knew him. He was a photographer, a good one. No I wasn't there to see him. I was there to see a girl who probably saw the police and ran. Ask my driver. I will go back to Beirut, but here is my card officer. Anything I can do to help. . . .

"Ah, Mr. Daoud. She is not there and you are a proud man. You are right, Mr. Daoud. Don't be sad, Mr. Daoud, you have lots of girls, pretty girls. The one in California is very pretty. . . ."

We were already on our way and the enormity of what had happened was catching up with me. "Abdel Karim, drive me to Beirut without one word. I am tired and upset and I don't want any fucking Lebanese monologues about love, women, honesty, generosity or any other thing you talk about a lot without having. Okay?" I frightened him, but not enough.

"Okay. I drive without one word, not even about the beautiful Lebanon mountains. You must admit, Mr. Daoud, Lebanon is a beautiful country."

In terms of our information needs, Sarkisian's death didn't matter. We had learned all we wanted to know about Syria's arms shipments to Lebanon.

Damn it to hell. I really hadn't bargained for that kind of work. To me, my relationship with Radio Freedom fell short of old-fashioned cloak and dagger stuff, and, though commitedly anti-communist, I didn't expect this type of savagery. I liked Sarkisian with all of his sad loneliness, his pathetic wish to identify with America, to belong, even as a traitor. I thought about how he had asked about his kids going to an American university and there was a big lump in my throat. Sarkisian, you silly old bastard, we had something in common, you and I. Come back so I can tell you the truth about America and the dream. Let me tell you what happened—what is happening—to mine. What a price to pay.

Yet I must admit that, even at this point of near incoherence, the ugly coin had another side. At the age of twenty-four, I felt an unexplainable type of youthful elation in the game, in being a spy. Sarkisian was killed and people didn't care. We had sought out a simple man with a wife and three children. We never contacted the family. Darrells had come back in time to arrange for the Lebanese police to leave me alone. This case and all the menace it created was my baptism in the ugly games department.

This would be a good way to begin with Anna, by telling her the story about poor little Sarkisian, or was the story about poor little me? Anyway, I had never told this story to anyone and getting rid of it would represent a first step towards telling the whole truth instead of the small parts of it which I had told to placate Maggie and feel better.

Here I was again, drunk at midnight, after my evening visit to the pub, wanting but unable to go back to sleep, remembering things fourteen years after the event and, damn it, it still hurt and wasn't real. What would I, if the chance ever presented itself, tell the children of poor Sarkisian? Well . . . that their father and I shared a desire to belong which translated into a strange affection for America because America institutionalized and annointed the craving to belong which all refugees have, even tone deaf Kissinger. This is rubbish, an attempt to intellectualize a poor excuse, the wish to belong.

What about the PLO assignment? What would I tell Anna about that? The Armenians are honorable, hard working people who would never accept a vague notion of a commitment to democracy to justify an act of treason. Damn democracy—it became the issue in hindsight. When all this happened, it had more to do with secret self-importance. Even the loneliness of it contributed to elation and was viewed as a positive element, an extra something which made for self-reliance and helped dilute the anguish and dull the moral senses. My protestations to Darrells against an anti-Palestinian assignment lasted five minutes, after which I moved forward ever so amorally to do what he wanted.

I will have to come back to this, to remember, to make mental notes, eventually to write and tell her or do it in person. Oh God! Oh God! How much I want to tell Anna. Oh God! How much I wish Anna was here. Not Emma, damn it, Anna. I want to hold her hand and say goodnight, just a simple goodnight. I wish she was here, near by, because she cared and understood. I didn't want to make love to her, only the comfort of her being with me and willingness to listen and share the heavy burden. Anna, Anna where are you? Even an Emma would do. Somebody, please. . . .

CHAPTER FIVE

Another whole day was wasted drinking and reflecting. The morning after was a return to routine, except the recently added anguish of Emma, Annabel's, Cape Miller and the footsteps had made it heavier than usual. The recollection of how it all started. I didn't think that was a bad sign, rather a good one. Perhaps, if it all came out, the rush towards destructiveness, the lack of caring, the loss of direction and the killer, the real killer, loneliness, might be answered, stopped. Who knows?

Putting all my remembrances of last night in a letter was out of the question. It would lead to here and now in no time at all and I wanted to delay that until the telephone calls clarified themselves or I came through with an answer. Perhaps now, perhaps they are waiting for me outside and if I walk around for a few minutes whoever is making the calls will make an appearance regardless of shape or manner. There is no danger; I am easy to eliminate so they must be after something else.

When my few minutes slow walk around the neighborhood produced no surprises, I went back home determined to keep the dialogue going with Anna—just in case, just in case I needed to use her for something.

Dear Anna,

I promised to write and here I am, at it again. Seeing you was great. It led to some looking back, perhaps the beginning of a march to where I am now.

In fact, I suspect you know more about the whole affair through your social circle—Felicity Broadcasting. Since you seem to think she is part of the problem, then I will correct that by breaking one of my old rules about kissing and telling.

I am not being pompous, but this isn't easy. I hanker for what existed between Maggie and me, for what was there before things went wrong because, for a change, it worked.

You knew and know me. We got together in spite of the colossal difference in our backgrounds. She was an establishment girl through and through, Roedean etc., but there was an odd craving for the exotic. After she had played at training as a secretary, she made vestments for priests, mended china, joined balloonists crossing the Channel and learned how to fly an airplane. For six months she was a stunt girl with an Australian movie company who still think she was the best. Because there was money, all of her efforts can be viewed as diversions, little fun things. Mind you, the family name and wealth were both used so discreetly, it took me years to know who they really were. She was introduced to me by a cousin about six years ago in a small clubby-type pub which catered for the elite of Knightsbridge.

Yes, she was tall, slim, blonde, pretty and had a background which showed—in her sober dress, the way she moved, the natural ease which is always inherited and seldom acquired. Something happened and we had eyes for each other, we were flirting.

Our first date was a disaster. She said very little while I carried on about everything under the sun. Anyway, the food was good, the wine, as one says, respectable and I got more pompous the more I drank—my usual way out. The end of our date found me shuffling my feet, unsuccessfully trying to produce ordinary social words to tell her how much I enjoyed the evening. She brought an end to my incoherent mumbling by making a good-bye sign and disappearing behind the door.

Our second date produced more exciting memories. A passing comment about twiglets looking like pretzels with a bad skin disease did the job; she fell over with uncontrolled childish laughter and we soon discovered that our appreciation of funny things extended to other matters.

With deliberateness, I asked her whether she could fill in for my secretary who was off on holiday to Austria. She said yes.

My naughty scheme took a long time to mature because Maggie came to work for me dressed like a regular Miss Smith and behaved the same way. My big, one room office forced some conversation, but she was hardly familiar and came and went like clockwork, for two whole weeks.

Then out of the blue she talked to me about saving a library of old Arabic manuscripts in Aden. "You should do something about getting all the Arabs throwing their money away to contribute some to The Royal Geographic Society." I couldn't help but inquire how come she knew so much about it and her answer deepened the intrigue. "I went there and saw it. Absolutely magnificent. I am trying to help them by raising money."

Our communications became a lot easier. I talked to her about the Bedouins and lamented the disappearance of their more noble traits while she reciprocated by discussing South America where part of her family lived, in Argentina. She mentioned that she had a sister and a brother and they sounded like the typical "well done, marvelous, good idea" types.

Yes, it was middle class chatter, innocent and unexciting, almost aimed at confirming normality and level-headedness, but it contained a subdued form of flirting while determining the rules of play.

Even now, recalling those little office conversations, I should have recognized the gulf which separated us. That's not true, I really still think of the finale as a bad dream and that one day I will wake up to a more pleasant reality—a friendly knock on the door. I don't know. I just don't know.

(I really can't bring myself to write this. All I know is that at the end of the last day temping for me she made me promise not to ask her to help again and we concluded things by having dinner then going to bed in a most natural uncomplicated way—the opening to five years of oneness which I still find difficult to talk or write about. Only what destroyed it can be described, is now beginning to be comprehensible.)

This tiring part is a start. Perhaps I will tell you more about her when I see you.

Love,
Daoud

This time, the waiting for a reply, the sense of expectation, wasn't as overwhelming as after my first letter. There was one short, silent telephone call from "them" at nine at night. A bit of a pattern about the time was emerging, either in the morning or at night, but nothing else changed. The day after, Anna called to invite me to her place and I accepted, looking forward to a much more relaxed atmosphere.

I reconfirmed that Anna had changed very little; time hadn't disturbed her figure nor her face. The only physical change I noticed was a few gray hairs which served a good purpose. She was still a handsome woman.

Yes, it was easier because it was later in the day and not improvised and having a drink came naturally. Being with an old friend was pleasant and enjoyable.

"I liked your letter about Maggie. She sounds like a nice lady! But tell me what you were killing yourself to keep inside—I mean tell me something about her, the real girl inside the outside girl."

"That's the way it was. A lovely girl, involved in odd things here and there, but very much the product of her class really, in most ways. Never gossiped, claimed it was the major sin of this country's upper class. At close quarters one of the finest minds I ever met, but totally mute if you got more than four people together—too shy to cope with groups. Spoke like a regular Sloane—except when we were alone."

Anna wasn't about to let go. "What got you together—besides ancient libraries?"

"Books, travel, theater, a common craving for knowledge for its own sake. I was like a father, a mentor, a guardian—she's ten years younger. When I first met her, her Miss Smith manner of dress had more to do with comfort than style. I changed that. I actually took her to Paris and showed her how lovely she looked when dressed elegantly—a cross between Charlotte Rampling and Susannah York. I introduced her to food, to wine and to a million other things."

"Christ, you're agonizing. Did you love her, Dr. Daoud Higgins?"

"Yes, I guess I still do. Not a weakness, I hope. But it was more. She was a good friend—much more than a sex partner, though that was okay. There was sharing, Cairo, Haiti, Oman and Turkey

35

and the little things one remembers. More to the point, I came clean, no pretense, to speak about me, my family and Bethany, the hard road to bloody Princeton and the uselessness of one night love stands. She knows more Bethany stories than I do. She genuinely loves them."

"Did you live together?"

"Yes, and no. She had her own place, but she was with me most nights, would come to see me early in the evening. She was most undemanding. I always wondered what her family said about our affair, but didn't ask and wasn't told. She always found something to do in my flat, something to improve— like a new flowerpot, a tie rack or even a medicine cupboard. She made it a home and I never had one. It's difficult to explain.

"Let's face it, Anna, my relations with women never completely worked, they were almost always contrived, distant. Suddenly there was enough to make every day a new one: sharing, enough for her to begin studying Arabic. To her, Arabic was the only thing which looked good in neon signs. Her only love letter to me was in broken Arabic."

"You don't have to tell me that you are distant. A bit arrogant with it, but never mind. I can see how she overcame that. She must have loved you. But what about your funny stuff?" Anna meant to unbalance me.

"What funny stuff?"

"Daoud, you started with Radio Freedom and you were valuable. I'm no fool. A *Time* magazine guy told me that in Nairobi last year, and he isn't the only one who gives you high grades. They don't let people like you go, RF and friends. She must have found out. Is that what you meant when you said she left because . . . is that why she left?"

My pause was overcome by a desire to accommodate Anna. "God, no. RF and friends, as you call them, are long gone. I left RF and all that in 1970 after a messy incident. Also, don't forget RF was the poor relation. We weren't the heavy boys, though it's still hush-hush. I really left, just quit. Let me take you out to lunch." I stood up.

"No need to bribe me. I want to listen to more nonsense about how you quit." Anna had done her homework.

"Yes, there is. Let's go to this new place, Ménage à Trois, in

Beauchamp Place and I will teach you how spies resign. See if you can get us a table. I understand it is rather difficult."

I moved around the place to stretch my legs as she went away and then came back to say that Ménage, which was around the corner, was all set, in fifteen minutes.

Ménage à Trois was a cosy little place. It specialized in tasty margaritas and we ordered two large glasses of the insidious stuff, after which we had a light chilled red Sancerre with our small portions of nouvelle cuisine and hot salads.

Soon we exhausted all conversation about the place and its food and were back to why I left the Middle East, after Radio Freedom, the final departure. I told Anna a story about when Maggie and I dined at Les Ambassadeurs with two old classmates, pre-oil money, from the prep school of the American University of Beirut. She had very seldom met people like them because normally I spent very little time with old friends from the Middle East. She said there was something good in me which surfaced in response to their presence, something decently Arab, while going back to America had reduced me to another number.

By the time we were back in South Audley Street, Maggie was hounding me with uncharacteristic annoying insistence. Why, she asked, did they think that I should have stayed in the Middle East? Why didn't I ever speak of the reason for leaving directly, and why did I always sound as if I was avoiding the issue?

"I was drunk, so I raised my voice at her with total exasperation and asked whether she really wanted to know. All of a sudden, completely out of character, her eyes widened and she said, 'My God, I have good reason to know everything. I have been around for four and a half years living every moment of your life and on the rare occasions when I meet an old schoolmate of yours I feel like a stranger. It all centers around that point, why you left the Middle East, why you emigrated to the United States! To me you have given loads of complicated reasons about America and the love of freedom, but to them you don't give that. Was there more to it?'"

"'Maggie,'" I said, "'Let's leave it to another time, it's a long messy story.' But this was not one of those occasions when asking for an extension worked.

"I remember telling Maggie nobody should know this, but I left the Middle East because I had to. I wasn't at all sure I would stay when I went back after college, but what happened made it impossible. I couldn't cope with the people there, oh no, no, no, not because they were Arabs. I hated the uselessness of the Arabs, still do. I hated the Arabs because they were me and they were crawlers, beggars. I hated the Arabs because deep down in their hearts they still played up to the colonialists.

"There was a long monologue after that about how the Arabs in power would look down on me because I was one of them and would have preferred to deal with one of my lowly blonde and blue eyed assistants if I had one. I was willing and able to deal with the Arab superficiality, cynically if only they would let me, if they would treat their own as normal people. On the other hand, there I was with Radio Freedom doing what I was doing and I didn't like that either, and though the Americans appreciated what I did, they never completely trusted me. I was really riding the fence. The Americans viewed me as an Arab and the Arabs viewed me as an American and the job that I was doing had one obvious reward—the feeling of being one of the masters, of being in with the Americans. That's why I left, that is why I left after the Radio Freedom assignment was over, though the parent company, the CIA, offered me a job. I turned down that God damn job. They really put me through shit. I went to work for Radio Freedom because of the little kid behind the wire fence in Eastern Europe and then slowly, meticulously they captured me, by playing on two things. It was interesting, exciting work, it produced an over supply of adrenaline, it made me feel important. You couldn't get around that feeling at twenty-three, dealing with things that changed the fate of the world. Oh my God, that's a dizzying feeling alright.

"To be honest about it, the second thing lives up to the famous cliché: once you're in, you can't get out. If you were like me and you were in, who would you turn to? Would you go back to the Arabs and tell them I have been working for Radio Freedom, the poor sister of the CIA and I want to get out! They wouldn't like that. They'd string you up and that would be the end of that. But then, you know, it was all little stuff and I was in the hands of a man called Darrells and it went from bad to worse. His requests were small at the beginning, then boom, we were into heavy stuff, for me conflict-making assignments."

I recalled all of these horrific, close to the heart things I had said to Maggie without stopping. Anna looked around the table to see whether the people were listening, but they weren't. They were preoccupied with the social season, races and balls, with all of the goody-goody stuff people at Ménage à Trois discuss. They weren't talking about the mental agonies of someone caught between two cultures, two loyalties. No, no, no, that was the thing farthest from their minds. Most of them weren't even talking about people. Horses came first, then the garden and oh, let's not forget about the weather. So Anna turned around and said, "Keep going, you're letting go at last and I want to hear more. Continue, please continue, and we can have another bottle of that lovely stuff."

"You know, Anna, the oldest and perhaps dirtiest intelligence trick in the world is undermining your opposition through releasing compromising information about them. Or turning them, making them cooperate with you because they have no choice. There are endless combinations and variations of what you can do with them once the blackmail works. You blackmail people most of the time by dealing with information of a totally personal nature, seldomly with things which have to do with spying. No, with people's lives, their families, their whoring, debts and friends — even the legendary alcoholic wife — which makes them security risks. This is old stuff which will work as long as people descend that low in the name of nonsense like country and honor and the preservation of Christian society.

"I didn't know why RF thought I'd be a good blackmailer or what prompted them, but ... well ... suddenly they went for some people, wanted them blackmailed. Sometimes they don't need intelligent reasons for what they do; they say they should have done it before."

"You're intelligent. Who did they go after?" She was more sober than I was.

"No, I am not. If I were I wouldn't be blabbing away in the middle of this place. I wouldn't be carrying on like this!" I moved my hands and came close to knocking the glass over.

"I think it's best if you do, don't you?"

I didn't answer. Of course it's best if I do, out loud. This is the perfect time, a no-man's-land between restrictive sobriety and loose incoherent drunkenness, the moment when drink has unlocked the mental vault and free expression is unencumbered by fear or care, when the mind can be relied upon in terms of total recall and clear organized presentation of the facts. We cross this narrow strip of delicious articulate inbetweenness fast and I must hurry because I've had a lot to drink which is moving me towards unreliable alcoholic discursiveness. Hurry Daoud, hurry damn it, tell her, hurry. The buzz in your mind is getting stronger so get a move on before she asks more questions and disturbs the balance. Now.

"That damned terrace of the St. George in Beirut ruined more lives than I could ever count. The place seated no more than thirty-eight people and I swear there were about thirty-eight anti-Arab plots a day. All that was missing was Sidney Greenstreet and Peter Lorre.

"Piss on that place and I don't care if you could see people water-ski and snow-ski in the same line of vision. It was a brutal place, the spot where East and West pretended they communicated with each other. The hell they did.

"Darrells needed that unblessed spot. He derived strength from it. Piss on it."

"Okay we'll piss on it. What happened there, Daoud?"

I took time out to empty my glass of wine then continued. "Well what happened was the height of absurdity. Listen to this. The US has always supported the Israeli position that Palestinians don't exist, that there is no Palestinian people. Then, out of the blue, good old Darrells wanted to know what the Palestinians were up to, what they were doing. How can people who don't exist do anything? This piece of logic isn't the work of a lanky queer from Urbana, Illinois, no, no, this piece of logic is part of US foreign policy. The Palestinians don't exist, but we must keep tabs on them, in this particular case penetrate them. We must keep tabs on them through other Palestinians who also don't exist—me!

"The idea that an organization representing the Palestinians would come into being frightened America. I mean look at the way they react to the PLO most of the time.

"On the surface, my brief was a simple one. Darrells wanted me to gather usable information on the leadership and direction of any Palestinian movement—immediately. It had to come from sources close to the top. We wanted to substantiate some rumors we had heard. The source, the parentage of the rumor, that is what we wanted.

"Don't ask me the obvious: where do the Israelis fit in? I have never figured it out. It gnawed on me, but eventually I told myself that I was dealing with saving the Middle East, something bigger than a narrow corner of it, the Palestinian problem. If you repeat these things to yourself often enough, either openly or secretly, then you begin to believe them.

"Who's blackmailable, vulnerable, is a problem, potentially a dangerous one. Sure I had contacts with Palestinian activists. I was close to some with whom I had gone to school. But there were so many of them, our thriving bureaucracy in exile rather than a government in exile.

"Darrells supplied me with a list of potential victims, about forty names altogether. Some were discarded because the time to check on them wasn't available, like the ones who lived and worked in Saudi Arabia. Others didn't qualify because they were not important. And there were the Mr. Cleans, the ones like George Habbash who may be called 'hoodlums' by foreign correspondents but who were beyond reach—no interest in money, women and no blemish on ancestry.

"My final list of candidates was down to ten or twelve people. Most of them were vulnerable because at some time they had received large sums of money in bribes, even well above what generous Arab protocol allowed. Others appeared to have mysterious, questionable personal connections and still others had relations who had made errors which history rendered fatal.

"The first man I approached had three qualifications. He was close to Palestinian activists, had high contacts with the Iraqi military establishment and a weakness for money. He was old-fashioned, insensitive and antipathetic, fat, with clammy hands and shifty eyes. We determined that the Iraqis needed pilotless drones and had made contacts with Italian, Canadian and Australian makers of such surveillance aircraft. All countries approached were willing to sell such units to Iraq, but all of them made it plain that they couldn't supply the necessary electronic gear. This needed US Government approval because it was American-made. To us that was an opening. Meridian Payne of the US made a drone with the equipment the Iraqis needed.

"I approached the haughty son of a Jaffa judge through a friend and pretended to be involved in arms sales. I told him I could reach Meridian Payne and suggested US approval for such a sale wasn't as difficult as envisaged. After all, drones carried no lethal weapons and the US was not averse to accommodating Iraq as long as no lethal weapons were involved. Since US laws forbid the payment of commission, I suggested the sale would be made through an offshore corporation which would order the planes on behalf of Iraq. There would be two sets of sales transactions and our payment would come from the offshore corporation whose books were beyond the reach of US tax inspectors.

"Our target, heaven's gift to Palestinian aspirations, one Banal Nagil, was ecstatic. He was to make three million dollars in commission, a hefty sum. The high level of commission was possible because no two reconnaissance planes were the same and commissions were high for dealing with unique products.

"We wrote a three page agreement covering the deal and our friend signed the agreement on every single page in both Arabic and English as was requested of him.

"A little time after, the Defense Department in Washington told Meridian Payne, a primary defense contractor, to write a letter to our friend 'regretting their inability to continue negotiating the sale' because the US Government had decided not to grant an export license. This was the end of my involvement, but it was just the beginning for Banal Nagil. Darrells told me everything was under control. The signed copies of the agreement would one day be useful.

"Seven years ago he was sent to New York as the first PLO spokesman to the United Nations. The whole world marveled at his eloquence and moderation. Little did they know of the major reason for the moderation. The US Ambassador to the United Nations dictated to the PLO man what to say. He told him about the US's desire to have him continue to 'behave'. Banal Nagil had been working for the US all this time, living in fear of exposure and our friend remains very much part of Arafat's entourage. He belongs to the 'moderate wing of the PLO', smokes cigars which cost eight pounds each and is in charge of PLO–Saudi relations. I don't think he's ever been near a Palestinian refugee camp in his life."

I avoided Anna's eyes by playing with the glass. "The second case was much easier. It really could have been avoided by the weak victim, a US-educated Ph.D. who was a lecturer at Kuwait University and who had a weakness for blondes and Black Label whiskey. He came from the small village of Beit Rafafa outside Jerusalem, had made himself a name and was a member of all the appropriate professional associations, the ones made up of the men of letters who told ordinary people what to do. The Palestinian members of these organizations were people who every once in a while forced their ideas on their fellow Arabs, who in turn advocated a stronger pro-Palestinian stance by their government and people.

"This weakling's misfortune didn't have anything to do with him or for that matter his father. It had to do with his grandfather. His grandfather, a sympathetic popular village head, had sold a piece of land to Jewish settlers in 1913. This land became part of a settlement which eventually was used as a military staging post, allowing the Israelis to occupy his home town of Beit Rafafa. This man's colleagues would indeed have disowned him. After all, Middle East society is still the family and the tribe, and if your grandfather committed a crime then you had to pay the penalty. To Arabs, blood is thicker than political commitment.

"I told the Beit Rafafa guy that we had documentation indicating that his grandfather sold the land to the Jews. His first reaction was: so what! My answer was the Arabs won't like it. He replied that no one would condemn him, but he knew better. When he finally got to what he could do for us, I told him that we would really like to have the minutes of the various meetings of the so-called Palestinian intellectual groups to which he belonged. They were scattered throughout the Middle East and as there was no Palestine within which to meet, they met in Kuwait, in Amman and Cairo. They met in other places also and called themselves one Palestinian organization or another and, believe it or not, the US monitored them. I told the man that our concern was not to undermine such organizations or any respectable Palestinian organizations because we believed their existence was healthy. The US Government, I insisted, realized that, but couldn't admit it because of the Jewish vote. Our concern, as I half believed myself, was to stamp out leftist and communist thinking from these groupings. Unlike the first recruit, my Beit Rafafa victim asked the obvious question: whether the information would be recycled and sent to the Israelis through the CIA. I assured him that as far as I knew it wouldn't.

"That was our big foray to keep the CIA books up-to-date. It was a long way from worrying about the little boy with the big black eyes to betraying my own people. That's why I wanted my three

year term to end so I could take the first plane out of the Middle
East and go as far away from it all as possible, to pretend that it
was nothing but a bad dream. You see, I was a victim myself, a man
unhappily in the middle being manipulated by sinister powers
beyond his control. I was as good as done from the moment I
innocently accepted the Radio Freedom assignment. Not much to
do after that. I couldn't even talk to my own father about it . . . to
anyone.

"The moment you commit treason, it is all the way. It is like
murder, qualitative not quantitative. How could I have known
what Radio Freedom was all about?

"America pushed me into this after it gave me Princeton,
washing dishes for a dollar an hour and a packet of free cigarettes
at Jimmy's Bar at night. America afforded me acceptance that I
never had in the Middle East. I had to go back to America to
rediscover its true values. I had to get out of the Middle East, to
escape the scene of the crime. I had to find a regular everyday
middle class job, perhaps live in a suburb with a wife and kids and
spend my weekends pottering around the house while drinking
beer. Perhaps it would require more: an atmosphere that would
allow me to reread the Gettysburg Address, yes the Gettysburg
Address.

"Now you know why direct, simple answers aren't easy. I never
wanted to tell this to anyone, but—it isn't an issue between us. It
really is better untold. Friends, would-be listeners can never help.
I wanted to rediscover America. There was something in that land
which is part of my free soul which I needed. I didn't want to put up
with new and vulgar Arab money. The Arabs didn't appreciate my
worth—never mind my ability. The Arabs need sycophants with
family background and I wasn't either. Damn the pigs. The first job
America offered me was a horrible accident and the scars . . . hell,
let's not talk about the scars. Enough. Christ, I've rehearsed this by
myself a hundred times and now it's out. Enough, no more. Just
more wine. I know there is no answer."

Anna sat listening, rapt. She was amazed at the flow of words
and refrained from calling them pompous. Certainly this was a
change from our previous meeting. Certainly I was letting go.
Certainly whatever had been bottled up was uncorked and
certainly, most certainly, I was feeling better for it.

It was when I spoke about ideas, she once told me, that light came to my eyes, that things changed. Maggie had said the same thing. Ideas and ideals and what they did to me, little tired, selfish me. I didn't know what to say or do next.

I looked at Anna. She had not missed a pause, a verb, a comma. She looked pained. She knew or felt what I had gone through, but she had no answer, and so I looked at her, put my head in my hands, waited a minute and then began to sob uncontrollably. For the first time I saw the people at the tables next to ours look at us as my body heaved and my words became unintelligible. I couldn't stop. I pleaded with her. "Anna, for Christ's sake take me home."

Her hand touched my shoulder and she walked me out after organizing the bill. She put her elbow underneath mine and led me into the street and eased me into a cab which took us to South Audley Street. Our slow climb up the stairs was punctuated by fits of sobbing on my part and when we reached the bedroom she undid my shirt to help take it off. I moved from one foot to the other to keep my balance and then I managed to unlace my shoes and took them off to be followed by socks and trousers which I threw on the floor before collapsing on the side of the bed and turning my back to her to continue to cry and moan. A small hand touched my forehead and a faint voice said, "Go to sleep now. Enough for a day. I will be here when you wake up. I'll go to sleep in the other room."

"Oh, my God, Anna, don't go away. Stay here. Please stay here with me."

The ringing of the phone paralyzed me into semi-sobriety and Anna noticed that I was watching her answer it, but she knew there was more to it than her simply answering the call. Anna stayed with me, for hours served me more drink and listened to more stories. I fell asleep trying to gaze at her in a way to say thank you, to say something beyond words, to apologize for the call—yes!

When I got up very early the following morning, she wasn't in bed, but I could hear noises from the direction of the kitchen and I found her there sitting at the small table playing patience with a deck of cards she had found somewhere. She was fully clothed, quiet and, uncharacteristically, wore a slightly bewildered look. I don't think she knew what to say, but she was ready to listen, or leave, or do whatever was required of her. The whole thing had been too much. Even after all the preliminaries, she wasn't ready for what eventually happened, and the telephone call capped it all. It was obvious that she had been awake for a long time.

We passed almost an hour in stilted, uneasy conversation, then I suggested that we go down to my Italian café. We passed by the Indian newsstand and picked up the newspapers, some cigarettes and the *Daily Telegraph* for her. She didn't ask any questions, nor did she provide me with the one answer I needed about what, if anything, she might have heard on the phone. As she left, she leaned over and asked me to telephone her in the afternoon.

The walk back home took place after the usual hour in the café. I moved around tidying up and busying myself, knowing that I was killing time waiting for the pub to open. Soon enough, the hour came, eleven, the mental chime for the regular walk to the Knightsbridge pub with all the same meaningless talk which repeated itself every day. It was a meeting place for losers. One habitué would never drink his beer without buttoning his jacket which only made him more boring. Why do I go there, I asked myself? Have I become boring? What was happening to me? Well, whatever it was, it wasn't boring. Hell, not that. I can't get my thoughts straight ... am I losing my mind, am I? Perhaps ... perhaps that's what they are after. They are trying to drive me mad. I need a drink ... a good stiff drink ... am I ranting ... no, no I need a drink, that's all, a drink.

CHAPTER SIX

The wavy whisper on the telephone line told me it was Beirut; it wasn't them, it was Papa. My initial worry about his long routine questions which betrayed a deeper concern was wrong. He was in a hurry to tell me that he was stopping in London for two days on his way to a meeting with his editors in New York, another boring review of the intractable Lebanese mess.

At Heathrow Airport four days later I was comfortable knowing that the dreaded personal conversation, the natural extension of his recent telephone inquiries, would be avoided for some time. Though he never admitted it, he hated flying and every plane trip produced a new story about a possible mishap and this expression of fear of flying would be compared with previous ones which were wedged in his memory. The review of imaginary accidents would be thorough. The details never changed, even in this he was consistent, and it would take enough time to get us to the Grosvenor House Hotel. After that it was all up to him.

Inevitably, something would have to be said about Beirut, the once beautiful city which trivialized bloodshed. But there was more room in family gossip, perhaps family affairs would occupy all our time—particularly with Jadi drinking again. Family drunks are always a long conversation which, like their drinking, repeats itself without solving anything. Well not to worry, there were lots of things to discuss before reaching me, hopefully without including me.

Just in case, I prepared to lead him into telling me stories about his youth, the amazing life he had led. He enjoyed that and managed to produce something startlingly new every time. Whichever way the conversation went, I decided that the other people at the arrivals gate weren't as lucky as I was. They weren't waiting for a natural story teller, or a legend in his own time, or for that matter, someone whose very being was enveloped in grace which transmitted itself to others. I was full of pride in him and shame of myself for having misgivings about his visit.

The big expansive Arab embrace had a special quality to it. We squeezed each other within it to confirm that it was love, to distinguish it from the everyday hugs and kisses which lost their meaning when the desert met the city. I pulled away from him while my hand was still in his and nodded in open proud respect, suddenly remembering what Maggie had said about him being the only thing I revered. She had been touched and elated by my outward manifestations of courtesy and respect because she too saw in him that rare majesty of presence.

I ushered him out of the airport into a taxi while in a happy trance. Yes, yes, Maggie, I really do love him and I should have done more than hug him with teary eyes, I should have gone down on one knee and kissed his hand three times, the way he kissed his father's hand and his father kissed his father's hand before, all the way back.

I left him alone at his hotel to unpack, clean, listen to the BBC World Service and telephone New York. I returned early that evening, sober. So far everything had gone according to my mental plan: comments on the poor maintenance in the Middle East of civilian aircraft, followed by agreement that the Lebanese were lunatics. His agile mind took this latter comment a step ahead and he allowed as to how the whole world must be mad because the conflict in Lebanon was a war by proxy and I agreed with this disquieting theory, as usual.

At the Chinese restaurant around the corner from the hotel, we made the usual passing comments about various members of the family until we got to my brother Jadi and his drinking which used a whole hour. He gave no hint that he knew about mine and I hoped that his restraint was genuine. Perhaps the abstinence of the previous two days showed me in a good light. We concentrated on Jadi and why an Omar Sharif handsome, exceptionally intelligent young man of thirty-two with a good job and a pretty wife drank so much. Of course there was no answer and we concluded with the usual expressions of familial concern.

On the way back to the hotel for an early night, I asked about Raouf whose absence from our previous conversation was conspicuous because Papa knew he and I were closer to each other than the rest. Papa said that Raouf was still doing "his own thing" and then uttering a sigh of admiration he added, "There is something disarming about people of commitment. We surrender to them even when we disagree with them because we envy them their sense of honor.''

I didn't go to see him until eleven the following morning; I wanted him to have a good rest. But as usual he was a step ahead, he had breakfasted and read all the Arabic and English newspapers and was ready to go. We agreed on a walk in St. James's Park because it was more like London, unlike Hyde Park it hadn't become unattractively international and was near the small, agreeable Italian restaurant where we wanted to lunch.

Because our way took us through streets full of antique shops and casinos frequented by Arabs, the walk was leisurely. Papa asked about the Arabs entering and leaving the casinos at that hour of the morning and when I recited the names of well known businessmen and politicians who used them he shook his head in utter, undisguised dismay. Gambling was his pet hate. He took singular exception to people betting against mathematical odds and dismissed talk of the sense of exhilaration which is supposed to go with it as nothing more than "a stupid justification for a stupid activity".

Suddenly, in the park, our conversation became disjointed. The amount of time we spent on any topic got smaller and smaller and the more difficult it became to maintain an easy dialogue the faster he walked. I had a hard time keeping up with him. Every sense I possessed told me that something was about to burst, that something within him was propelling him towards uncharacteristic behavior.

He had moved two steps ahead of me and I beheld him for what he was, a slightly stooped, somewhat overweight, formless cuddly figure, the way they all become at his age. But there was a certainty in his step that defied his years and certainly his mind had been sharpened rather than dulled by time; it ranged with healthy youthful inquisitiveness. He slowed down to allow me to catch up with him and, involuntarily, his right hand reached for his head and he scratched it the way he always did when mother became unreasonable and there we were next to each other knowing that the hour of reckoning wouldn't, couldn't, be delayed.

Preparedness doesn't make for an easy confrontation, I told myself, as he passed his hand through his hair two more times as if to confirm his reluctance to begin. He looked straight ahead and so did I. I waited.

"Daoud, as you know I've never told any of my children what to do, how you should conduct your lives—not even Jadi and God knows he needs some talking to—but I would like to ask you a question if you don't mind." At this point, he turned into a path which cut across the whole park and slowed down a bit more.

"Of course I don't mind, Papa. You can ask anything you want any time. I hope you know that." I tried to sound normal, but he couldn't; he actually cleared his throat.

"What happened along the way, son? What happened to you along the way?"

"I don't know what you mean, Papa. What is supposed to have happened along the way? I am a little tired; I've been working nonstop since college and it's time for a little rest. Money isn't a problem. Nothing really happened, nothing."

He interrupted. "Bear with me a moment, old people and children have problems putting thoughts together. I'm not talking about money—not even about work, really. I think you know what I am talking about. You're not where you should be, where you wanted to be and where I hoped you would be. Something happened to you and you are unhappy. We both know it."

I caught a glimpse of him biting his lower lip. God, he only did that when she hounded him with her haughty, unreasonable requests. It was a literal gesture; he didn't want to say anything that would hurt, but he still continued.

"You're all my children. I love you all, but in your case what a waste. Nobody expected much from Jadi, but you're different. Even mother thought you'd make it all the way and God knows she finds it hard to part with praise. She enjoyed hearing about your work with the people in Iraq, though I didn't. Nothing more than thugs and gangsters pretending to speak for the people. You're not up to them, son. They're scum." For a moment he choked.

"Well Papa, sometimes I think it's unfair to expect things from others. I know you're right about them . . . you're right. But then I am grown up and have to live with my own decisions. Nothing happened to me, not really, though I discovered that I don't like people. Perhaps it's people. The way, as you call it, is a meandering stream; it leads to many places. There's time; lets see what happens after a little rest. . . ."

I was crying for him to stop and for a brief moment I thought he had. No, the compulsion reasserted itself. "What about Maggie? Most of your girlfriends have been nice ladies, but she was special.

I liked her very much the two times I met her. Solid stuff and also very sweet. Did she have anything to do with your quitting work? Where is she now?"

"God, no. Maggie is a true Brit though different in many ways. No, she didn't cause this. I am glad you liked her; she was extremely fond of you, Papa. She actually came to life when you were here, loved your stories. Maggie is with her parents, I hear. Yeah, a nice lady but the odds were against it. Too much to overcome. She belongs to another world." This time I could hear my voice getting thick and he let me off the hook as I was trying to steady it.

"I'm sorry things aren't right, but I am not going to ask any more questions. I can't even answer these things myself. Looking back, I wonder whether it was all worth it? I stopped fighting sometime back and settled for small steps, doing some good here and there. I suppressed my anger. You and Raouf are angry; you're at war. Still, his way makes him happy and yours doesn't. Sure, there is a lot to be angry about, a hell of a lot, including the clowns who go to casinos in the morning."

Wishing to avoid a response to a lament which sounded like a plea for compliments, he changed the subject by pointing to a modern building near Buckingham Palace. "Why in God's name did they allow them to build that one over there? It's American and out of place . . . ghastly."

Slowly he eased the talk into comments about life in London. We had gone around the park, oblivious to other people around us, and except for my occasional make-believe football kick of twigs which cluttered our way, we had been totally engrossed in ourselves, a deliberate, painful look into whether our lives made any sense. The timing of his complaint about the modern building may have been contrived, but the emotion was genuine. He liked the Brits and things British because he knew what they stood for and that contrasted with his feelings towards the Americans— what he called "boisterous uncertainty".

What a man, I thought to myself after we had lunched and separated for an afternoon rest, what a truly remarkable man. He had a knack of seeing around corners, of determining things before they occurred and he incorporated all he saw into a body of judgment which never lost its vigor. Certainly he knew things were wrong with me, very wrong, and that pained him, but he was too gentle a man to say more than he did. He settled for telling me that he loved me and I agonized over my inability to say the same. I wanted him to know.

That night, an inadvertent restaurant tour found us in a Lebanese restaurant where we decided Lebanese food was better in Beirut, closer to its roots. We skipped from one light conversation to another and had much fun talking about my nephews and nieces who, naturally, were all geniuses. Not a word about earlier that day, nothing more to confirm either our love or our separateness.

Papa was anxious to be in New York the following day. He insisted on paying for dinner and announced that he would go to the airport alone, that there was no need for me to accompany him at such an early hour.

The time to say good-bye at the hotel was an immersion in pain. When old people take leave from us, we always wonder about seeing them again, and in this case I wished that our time together had been longer and different, but I knew that it had to end this way. All the things I wanted to say to him were reduced to "Don't make it too long, Papa. Come back soon. Don't make it too long." Again we avoided each other's eyes.

I returned to South Audley Street, determined to have a long night's sleep. I felt tired, drained and very edgy. The man's natural gentility had demanded a like response from me; the careful use of words, the unmarked boundaries beyond which he didn't tread and the reality of it all—the total absence of guff. I poured myself a big slug of vodka to guard against too much tossing and turning later, to ease the proxy confrontation with Papa.

The telephone rang a moment after I got into bed as I was contemplating the desirability of another vodka. Christ, it was another empty one. I had almost forgotten about them and the lack of expectation helped. "Listen you silly bastard, I am not the type who frightens easily. I think I know who you are." And while the wire remained live, "I am getting tired of this, either you speak and tell me what you want or you're going to have to deal with my kid brother, Raouf."

The click penetrated the innermost part of my head. God, they responded to his name. Holy God, they knew Raouf. They knew my little brother.

CHAPTER SEVEN

Papa's brief visit unbalanced my routine. His comments and the huge divide which separated us had become part of regular mental tours. He, Maggie and Raouf were the loves of my life, but remained very much outside it. There was an order to their lives while mine was in suspense, refusing to provide the answers I was demanding from it. The destructive examination was occupying me the way work had done; it had become a substitute for normal activity and life had become a mosaic of compulsive masochism.

The ring of the door bell caught me half way down the stairs on my way to the pub and for nearly five seconds I didn't know whether to climb back to the landing and buzz the visitor in or to run down to the door or even to ignore it altogether. I decided to confront the unknown caller.

The man facing me was Middle Eastern, around fifty years old, heavyset with thick, long, straight, black hair. He looked as if he had come directly from Savile Row. The ordinariness of the gray color of his suit didn't detract from its quality and the off-white silk shirt and impeccably knotted tie added to a picture of a worldly man of style. He was deliberate and very quick, but neither jumpy nor agitated, putting forward a heavy, strong hand with enviable assuredness. "Mr. Daoud, I am Dr. Raji. Sorry to come like this. May I come in, please?"

"How do you do, sir. Of course, come up. I am afraid it's a wretched climb. I will lead the way."

I moved up the stairs steadily, two steps ahead of him. No, there was no fear; he wasn't the killer type—much too important for that. Fifty year olds seldom, if ever, kill, and besides you couldn't adopt his manner of dress just for an assassination; his dress was part of his character. This man had come to talk business, whatever it might be. He wasn't even the type who'd make empty telephone calls. "In here, Dr. Raji. This is my humble office. I am afraid I don't have mint tea, but how about some coffee or diet Pepsi. I pretend I am dieting." I tried to smile.

He sat on the leather sofa facing the desk, moved the flaps of his jacket out of the way, clasped his hands on his crossed knees in formal informality and asked for a soft drink.

I waited for him to say something, but he deliberately busied himself with the iced glass of Pepsi by twisting it around.

"This is indeed a surprise, sir. What can I do for you, Dr. Raji?"

"I am from Iran."

"Yes." I had already recognized the accent by its heaviness and the slowness of speech.

"I wanted to meet you. You are Palestinian. . . ."

"Yes, I am Palestinian-American." I sat facing him from behind my desk and stared right back at him.

"Yes, I know you have an American passport."

"Well, I am a little more American than that."

"I noticed the buttoned down shirt. I went to Cornell myself briefly, but never mind that. You are Palestinian."

"Yes, I can't deny that and don't want to deny it, but tell me more, Dr. Raji. This is all unexpected."

"We are friends of the Palestinians."

"Yes." I dragged out the word, hoping to convey my exasperation only to discover that he was feeling the same way.

"Mr. Daoud, I must leave London tomorrow. I don't have time to waste. I want to speak to you very seriously."

"It seems we are already speaking seriously."

"Mr. Daoud, are you still working for Iraq?"

"No." I was determined to remain totally immobile, to wait for him.

"Are you working for the CIA?"

"Never did."

"Mr. Daoud, we know a lot."

"If you do, then you should know I never did. I worked with them—never for them. If you know a lot, then you should know that."

"Alright, are you working with them now?" And this time there was a flicker of a smile.

"No."

"I believe you."

"Believe me or not, that's the way it is." You are going to give in before I do, you bastard.

"Would you like to help us, Mr. Daoud?"

"Dr. Raji, to put it in the vernacular, it's the best offer I've had this week, but if you are talking about the present government in Iran, then the answer is no—even though I don't know what helping you means." Come on Doctor, you're dressed to represent a government, not a revolutionary group.

"Don't be in a hurry to say no. There are a lot of reasons why you should. . . ."

"I can't, as an American. Much more importantly, I can't as a person. I could never justify it to myself. I'm against the reversion to religion. Among other things it would interfere with my drinking." And now we both smiled.

"Mr. Daoud, I am very serious. It would please your brother if you cooperated with us. He believes that we want to go to Jerusalem. Where you came from, isn't it near Jerusalem?"

"Raouf! Raouf is my brother and I love him, but he goes his way and I go mine."

"He is a good man."

"Sure he is. We are very close, except when it comes to politics."

"Do you believe that we want to go to Jerusalem, to liberate Palestine?"

"Perhaps." My God, aren't you tired of this, I thought.

"Do you speak German, Mr. Daoud? I find it easier to speak German. I got my Ph.D. there. I am a banker. I was a banker under the Shah and I am still a banker. I'll probably be a banker if a new government takes over, but—whoever it is—governments change, but some of us don't. I serve my country." At last he was beginning to move.

"Dr. Raji, if I spoke English as well as you do, I'd use no other language. I understand and appreciate what you are saying, but I don't know what I could do to help you and I'm not at all sure I want to find out."

"Would you listen if I told you?"

"Yes, provided you tell me who you represent."

"The Prime Minister and the Islamic Economic Organization. This Organization is more important than the Government. We control what matters, the money." Dr. Raji spoke for five information-packed minutes about a shadow government in Iran, a group very Islamic in outlook but determined to rid the country of confused religious hysteria and committed to redirecting it towards "political and economic sanity".

"Well, I am glad there is something sensible in the wings beside your present Government or Governments. You've got people confused as to who runs the show! What is the Organization all about politically? What is your major aim?"

"Jerusalem."

"Dr. Raji this all sounds nice—people have been giving us Jerusalem on a daily basis and I enjoy sparring with you—but you have to be very clear with me as to why you came to me, who you are, and what you and your organization want in addition to Jerusalem." But even my leaning on the desk and staring at him didn't seem to phase Raji.

"I have no problem being specific. My name is Dr. Raji Sheth. I am the Chairman of both the Bank of Samahure and of the Islamic Economic Organization and I am a close friend of the Prime Minister. Our Organization wants, through control of Islam's wealth, to perpetuate the commitment to liberate Jerusalem. We must end all our feuds with our Moslem brothers. I came to see you because we know how effective your work for Iraq has been. We need arms: SAM 7s, Stalin Organs, Haag Missiles and much more. We want an honorable end to the war. We know we cannot win while America is against us, while they supply the Iraqis with blueprints to build chemical warfare plants. Most of the arms we need come from Russia. Russia is already selling to Iran. We want to get in the middle, get a commission on all their sales there so that the Organization can continue to work towards the liberation of Jerusalem through supporting Islamic groups in Lebanon, Egypt, Saudi Arabia and elsewhere."

"Sounds like an Islamic United Jewish Appeal dabbling in armaments."

Grinning just a tiny bit, Dr. Raji continued. "It's no joke, Mr. Daoud. It is very serious business."

"So is getting money out of the Russians."

"Not so, that's easy."

"No, no. Getting money out of the USSR is never easy."

"We can arrange the Russian money. We will make you a purchaser, an official representative. You pay them and have the goods shipped to us. The difference between what you pay and what we pay you is for the Organization."

"Is that the money going to Hizbollah and the bad boys?"

"No. Mr. Daoud. The money is for the long term, for groups who can assume power in these countries. Hizbollah can't."

"Dr. Raji, why me?"

He leaned back in his first physical move because he wanted this to sound important. "You can deal with the Russians and with the banks. You have a trading company. Your background makes you acceptable to both sides. You know about arms. You come from Jerusalem, so you should appreciate our purpose. You meet all our requirements. Later we want to use you for other things. We know you know the big French and British arms companies. We believe you agree with us. Didn't two of your uncles die fighting for Jerusalem in '48?"

"Yes, Doctor, they did. I loved them both."

"Help us, Mr. Daoud. Help us get to Jerusalem." My God, he was the real article, the Doctor. He meant what he said.

"You know how to make it difficult, Doctor, don't you! You know what Jerusalem means to me—to all of us, I guess. But Doctor, I don't believe in stoning people to death and I don't believe in suicide bombers and I am Arab and American. Also, I am not an arms merchant. I guess I was an ideologue trader; I bought arms for Iraq—though I had misgivings about Saddam. I don't hate them, though they disappointed me. Right now, all I want is to be alone. I can't believe my expertise is needed. Perhaps my brother misled you."

"Mr. Raouf doesn't lie or mislead. His only purpose in life is to go to Jerusalem. He helped us before the Shah's downfall; his group gave us seventy thousand Kalashnikov rifles and he trained some of our boys. Our aims are the same. He is a lovely man."

"Yes, I guess he's totally committed. I admire him, but I cannot agree. And, Doctor, we've known each other for only one hour and we're already talking about changing the map of the world. I cannot help, personally. But if you, that is your economic group, are a shadow government, then why not approach the US? They'd help as long as you are right wing and more likely to be a thorn in the side of Russia on a long term basis."

The signal to press the attack came when I noticed the Doctor considering his answer. "Unless there is something standing in the way ... something beyond the atmospherics. Is the chemical warfare plant problem a stumbling block? I thought the Germans were the ones."

"No, no. The plans, the blueprints came from the US, from a company called Zeitsler in Rochester, New York. They were obtained by an Iraqi named Dr. Kalam Zayed. Then he bought the various components from Germany and Italy and built the plant. The Americans supplied the vital part."

"Who is Dr. Zayed?"

"He's in jail now. He disagreed with Saddam on something. He worked with the Americans."

In spite of all efforts to control my reaction, I was breathless. "Doctor, this is heavy stuff. Are you absolutely sure?"

"Yes. We have pictures of Zayed and the head of Zeitsler in a Paris nightclub and other places."

"Let's backtrack a bit, Doctor. Do the Americans know that you know? I have to know whether you've already told them."

"We sent them a man, but they don't believe him. Can you help us convince them?" Yes, Doctor, this all rings true, I said to myself.

"Doctor, this is all insane. We've just met, but I am beginning to see what you're after."

"I don't have time, Mr. Daoud. Iran doesn't have time. We need air defense systems. The Iraqi Air Force killed over forty thousand people last month alone. They intend to use deadlier chemicals and it will get worse—perhaps biological weapons. We must end this war strong and then start working for the ultimate goal."

"Doctor, if the problem is getting the US to listen to you, how do I reach you? Where do I reach you?"

"In Tehran. My telephone number is 424 355."

"Use the phone?"

"Yes."

"No, no. What about by DHL?"

"Okay, PO Box 3437Z2512/16." He sounded as if he had memorized it especially for the occasion.

"That's a long number, why?"

"Never mind. Will you contact me?"

"Yes—regarding US interest, not mine. I am curious myself!"

"Okay. And Mr. Daoud, you are being watched."

"I know. Probably the people who told you my flat is on the second floor. A little more than watched, I think. I think my phone is monitored and other types of nonsense." I tried to be dismissive.

"I should think all that. . . . Don't think it's us, but perhaps— thank you very much, Mr. Daoud, it's nice to have met you."

"Dr. Raji, I will be in touch. I can't promise more. I will transmit your message as soon as possible."

"Thank you, Mr. Daoud, I know you will."

The Doctor held my hand in both of his strong hands and squeezed it while looking in my eyes and then erectly walked out of the room and headed down the stairs. The Doctor was for real. He was telling the truth, but that wasn't the problem. The problem was what to do with the truth, where to go. Not to Darrells, not him. Perhaps to Brandt or perhaps to the loud idiot who's always on TV here. Not him—he's messy—and this is big. The Doctor was in a hurry and he was aiming higher than local spooks at the Embassy and Middle East has-beens. To Brandt, this should go to Brandt—after the pub, when I come back at 3:00 p.m.

I arrived at the pub at 1:30 to be greeted by "You're late" cries from the regulars and a sly smirk from the owner. Someone bought me a drink. Unlike other times, ignoring the habitués' chatter wasn't deliberate. I kept drifting away thinking of my opening line to Brandt, going back to how we parted and trying to assess his reaction to my reappearance. Brandt was polite and cool, and always looked as if he was about to say, "Talk to me Daoud, I understand". Maybe this would do it, open the door for the personal bit, the heart-to-heart talk Brandt's manner always promised and which I wanted because Brandt knew the business and somehow he knew me. Time to go home, time to call Brandt, time to say talk to me and tell me what the hell has been going on.

I reached home a little after 3:00 p.m. and telephoned the Trikings Institution and after giving my name asked for Bill Brandt. He behaved as if he had been waiting for my call. "Daoud, how nice to hear from you. I've been meaning to call to see how you are, but we're so busy with everything that's going on. How are you?"

"I'm fine, Bill, just fine. Not doing much, but all is in place. Bill, listen to me very carefully because I don't trust the instrument in my hand, though friend Darrells isn't bothered by it."

"Go ahead."

"Someone from the other side, from the big country, came to see me this morning. He was straight and to the point. They want to talk. I believe the guy. I think my instincts are right."

"Your instincts are usually good. Can you tell me who it was?"

"A Dr. Raji. He claims."

"I know Raji. Didn't know they were using him. How clever of them . . . how very clever." The words were dragged out to allow him time to think.

"I can't say more this way."

"Don't. Let me call you back. Are you at home? You'd better let me have the number. Okay, I'll call you back."

My thoughts didn't center on whom Brandt would talk to, they were simpler ones that had to do with me and why I couldn't resist being involved again. Maggie was right, or almost right. It was my way of life. Dr. Raji recognized that. Bill Brandt knew it, but also noticed the inner restlessness, and Maggie was humiliated when she realized it came ahead of her, that my desire for recognition was stronger than my love for her. When the telephone rang, I was in the middle of trying to find a label to describe myself, but that could wait. Brandt was on the telephone. This was a new ball game.

"Hello."

"Daoud, listen, we want you to come over. I can't fly to London and I don't think you want Darrells there. Can you spare the time? Of course we will take care of everything." He sounded as natural as if he had been inviting me for a drink around the corner. But who did he talk to? Who decided Dr. Raji's lead should be pursued?

"Sure. I guess tomorrow at about noon. If you don't hear from me, then I am on my way."

"Go to the Four Seasons Hotel. Go there directly and call as soon as you get in. The room will be arranged."

"By the way, I fly first class. I hope bureaucracy won't object."

There was a chuckle on the other end and Brandt said that they all flew club class, but that it would be alright for me to fly first and we said our uneasy good-byes.

I hung up feeling better. That strange old feeling was back, the adrenaline was flowing; it was like being resurrected. Talk to Anna while I was in that frame of mind, on a high. I telephoned her and she answered instantly. Perhaps she had been waiting for my call.

"Hello, you asked me to ring the other day," I said.

"Yes, I did. I really didn't know what to say that morning with all those people around us. The whole thing was too much. My God, you have been storing it all up for a lifetime. But listen, why is it bothering you all of a sudden and why has it taken you days to call? What's happening now? What you told me sounds like ancient history—on the surface—if you have been away from it all for so many years. Has anything new happened? You told me what happened when you were in Beirut, but come on, that's a long time ago. I've been thinking. . . ."

"I know. I can't put one past you. They came back. They never really leave you alone when they need you. This time it's worse."

"Who came back? When?"

"Oh, not too long ago, about a year ago," and silently, dishonestly, I thought of today and the Doctor and couldn't understand why I gave her an opening.

"What the hell do you mean, they came back? Who are they? Stop it."

"Oh, it's not the kind of thing I want to talk about on the phone."

"Well, why didn't you tell me about it the other day?"

"I shouldn't tell you about it. I think I have bothered you enough."

"I just can't believe this, I really God damned can't. Come over now, come to see me. Let's continue this and get to the bottom of things. I'm beginning to understand."

"No, Anna, no more."

"Come on you idiot, you've told plenty already. Stop it."

"No Anna, no, no, no, no. Enough is enough. But tell me, the phone—they're probably listening now—what did you hear?"

"Forget the phone. Just come over. You only remember it when it's convenient. Just take a taxi."

"No, no, no, I don't want to do that. But I must know about the call the other night, I'm in a hurry."

"It played back a conversation between you and someone else, a telephone conversation."

"Christ himself, Anna. They sure are listening to us now. Why didn't you tell me?"

"I thought you knew. I thought it was what was bugging you. Come over and tell me about it. What does it mean?"

"Well . . . let's not talk about it now. Do you understand?"

"I thought we were alright last time. We were talking like friends when we started."

"Of course we were, but I don't want a repeat performance."

"Listen, you silly fool, don't become pompous and dramatic. Just take a taxi and come over. Remember, I do already have an idea of what's going on, but you do sound much better."

"No, no, no, but thank you. Thank you very much. I'll be in touch so don't worry about it, but don't call for now. I'll be in touch soon."

"Bye you, and listen, the telephone number isn't going to change. I'm still here."

"Anna, bye for now—you know what I mean!"

"Bye."

The talks with Brandt and Anna had drained me, especially Anna. I found myself tired after talking to her. The words didn't come out clearly, a tiny bit slurred and confused. Anna wouldn't mind. After all, there was no hiding it; I was drinking too much and she knew it. That was not anything to hide, no, no that wasn't the problem, just a manifestation. What bothered me right then was that Anna had become involved. Not only had I given away so much, but after all of the deliberations about keeping her out of it and how to talk to her, that was not the way I wanted things. My restaurant scene came out so badly, so messily and that was the fear, the way things came out. Then the part I wanted to hide by talking only about the past didn't last long. Now, whatever it was she had heard, the telephone caller had her on his list. So that was behind the accusing look the other night, the one with no sympathy . . . poor Anna.

Time to go to bed. Perhaps a little bit of rest, perhaps a little bit of reading if I try hard enough. Then after that back to the pub and a repeat performance of what happens every night. Or, on the other hand, it might just be slightly different. It could be that I will find someone with whom to play backgammon. They introduced the wretched game into the pub and everyone has been playing it. It is antisocial really, but then it's a diversion from repeating the same stories and reliving the same exaggerations. Oh my God, the ticket, the ticket to Washington. I'll arrange it for twelve tomorrow. I'll tend to the phone after that.

CHAPTER EIGHT

The promises to Anna were the ultimate dishonesty because I had no intention of telling her the real truth. You can't fool the Annas of this world for very long. If it hadn't been for the accident at the Ménage, she would already have decided that she was being used and would have objected by categorically demanding the truth or telling me to take my game and go to hell. She was capable of both.

I must be careful to separate what I am truly telling her from the shadow conversations I was having with her, my attempts to get a hold of what is happening through examining the past. Perhaps I should use Maggie's image for the mental reviews, but there is a big problem in using Maggie because love is blinding, even with hindsight.

I guess I can avoid the confusion by using someone else. After all, there were many of them, all abstract statistics until Maggie, all vague, pleasant social memories which, as Anna said, never got close. Maggie . . . Maggie got close. Maggie was always very close, as close as that night when she used her shyness gesture, the index finger in the mouth.

"Are you going to teach me everything you know?"

"Of course I will, anytime you're ready."

"Don't tease me. I'm ready now, but please, nothing rude, just something fun."

"Do you love me?"

"Yes."

"Maggie, do you really, truly love me?"

"Yes."

"Then keep your eyes open and look at me, be with me. There is nothing better than doing it together."

The cover of the bed was kicked away. I reached down and took off her socks and my hand climbed up the side of her body, all the way to her cheek, down to her breast and firm nipple and I leaned down and kissed her briefly and gently. We touched and touched, then we clinched to each other and I moved underneath with her on top and me inside her. I asked her not to move, just to look at me and tell me how it felt. My throbbing was answered back; we stared at each other while our fingers were entwined. We moaned with joy, trying to make the fit more perfect, the fierce squeeze of fingers bordering on pain. "Now, darling, now with me . . . oh God, it gets better all the time."

She collapsed on the bed in a state of delicious exhaustion, a moment of reverent silence.

"Can we do that again? Sometime soon!"

"Of course."

"I want to do it better, if that is possible."

I tapped her on the head with my index finger, smiled and accused her of being greedy.

"I want to be greedy when it's us. I hope you've never done this with anyone else."

"I promise, never the same with anyone else."

"Ain't I a lucky girl. I really love you." We had embraced.

Don't torment yourself, Daoud. Leave Maggie alone boy. Go down to the pub. Tuesday is a good pub day. The funny Cambridge-educated old man would be there, the specialist in superlatives. A retired army major to boot. Yes, Tuesday was one of his days.

I was right, Major Robert Gratt was there standing alone in a corner with a rolled magazine held firmly in his left hand. His aged, old-fashioned suit and manner always set him apart from the others and on this particular occasion he was hovering around a beautiful blonde who couldn't have been a day over twenty. The dirty old sod specialized in dizzy broads and he introduced me to today's lovely and launched one of his monologues, the usual endless exaggerations which embarrassed people away from him.

"Dear you, I haven't seen you in ages and ages. I was telling Liz about you. Our Liz is a model. I told her you were very big in advertising in New York, knew everyone in the business, everyone. Perhaps you could get dear Lizzie some work with people you know here, with your friends at Tates and Co. As the Americans say, they are the Cadillacs of the business. Dear Daoud went to Princeton. Forget about Harvard and all the rubbishy places. It is the best university. What is the name of the big white club on top of the hill? Someone wrote a beautiful song there.

Anyway, Lizzie can come to see you to show you her portfolio. She's done some work already."

Little Lizzie didn't say anything, no words passed her parted lips, just the implicit promise that she was willing to return any favor. I couldn't get out of promising Lizzie to check with advertising friends about possible jobs for her, but I emphasized that I had been away from the business too long, that I had left it and New York six years before and moved to London to set up a Middle East consulting business. Lizzie's lips remained parted.

Major Gratt and Lizzie worked while they lasted. Back to South Audley Street. Unsteady after the many drinks in the pub, I began to worry about next day's trip. Christ, I told myself, I'm going to be a mess if I don't sleep. Perhaps I should call Anna again. No, no, not after refusing to go to see her. I must prepare my suitcase and have a good night's sleep. Also, I must write to Anna. I must continue the holding action by writing, without drama and without sobbing in public. Perhaps I will continue and tell her some of the truth. I can't tell her all. Perhaps shit. I rolled from side to side uncomfortably. Perhaps the cold sweat would stop; it was making the sheets damp and uncomfortable. I felt filthy, both in body and mind. Promised myself to stop going back. I had no intention of telling Anna or did I want to? But it is so God damn long and complex. Nothing else could enter my mind. Nothing really, except what to tell Brandt. Would he believe the Doctor just knocked on the door? My head ached. Yes, Anna, I will write. You should know. If writing will help, then I will start tomorrow. I promise I will Anna, I promise. Tears rolled down. Jesus, how can I cry alone, without outside stimulus? Well, that's why I must write it down—perhaps purge myself of it. Yes, that's a promise, tomorrow before the pub opens. I mean on the plane, on the plane to Washington to see Brandt, with a ball-point pen . . . yes . . . yes.

My dear Anna,

I made a strange promise to myself last night. As you are part of it, I had better tell you about it right away. I am going to get everything off my chest, I am going to tell you the rest, bring you up-to-date.

Don't worry—it's impossible to do it all in one letter. It would be the longest in history. I will do it in pieces, one theme at a time to avoid making it complex. If this is going to be the honest, open effort I mean it to be, then I will start by admitting my own selfish reasons for writing it. I need to busy myself, to reinstill a measure of discipline which will reduce my time at the pub and other drinking spots. There is the broader need for a total review of what happened which could be of more lasting help. It might allow me to get a grip on myself and start me on the road back to normality—whatever that is. It is therapy—the only one I can think of, short of seeing a shrink which goes against the grain.

Let's talk about the immediate past for a change. Until four months ago, it consisted of two parts: Maggie and my consulting working, both gone now. I don't want to write a manual of puppy love, but it really was a special relationship. We belonged to each other in a total, self-contained way, didn't see anyone else. We enjoyed the same things and Maggie traveled with me whenever time and money allowed, which was often. Our life belonged to us and it was centered around us and the things we did. We exchanged presents on a regular basis and hugging and holding hands mattered as much as the real thing.

The only thing I knew about Maggie's family was that they lived in Wiltshire, had some money and that her father wrote loads of letters to The Times *which were never published. She knew everything about my family because she was interested in Arab lore and I acquainted her with stories about Bethany and all that, including how my dim-witted great-grandfather always rode the mule backwards. We decided that this odd compulsion was the equivalent to writing letters to* The Times; *he wanted to be noticed.*

Our relationship carried on while exciting, challenging developments were happening in my work. As you know, the Americans sent me to London to run the international consulting subsidiary of the big advertising firm. After two years, I gave it a Middle East tilt because I knew the area and lots of people in it. Then, realizing I didn't need the Americans, I set up on my own. I was a natural middle man, someone who understood both sides—then and now a rare commodity.

My Middle East client list was varied, but the jewel in the crown was my work for the Iraqi Government. A former classmate of mine had become Deputy Minister of Planning in that country. He was a sensitive, aware man whose work was to assess the massive development plans being adopted by his Government. The results of his studies produced the disturbing conclusion that "the most qualified" companies in the world weren't working in Iraq for an obvious reason: the country had a bad image overseas, particularly identification with terrorist movements. Surely something had to be done about enticing good corporations to work in Iraq, and it had to be done more subtly than through the existing incompetent and suspect Iraqi Government commercial offices overseas.

Nobody else was better qualified to do the work needed for the Iraqis than someone like me. I knew more about Iraq than most, I knew the communications business including valuable contacts in the press, and had connections with the relevant major corporations as well, along with an appreciation of what made them tick. Not only did Iraq want better companies with which to cooperate, but their policy suggested an opening to the West and a shift away from Russia.

It was fun and genuinely exciting work for the most promising country in the Middle East, though I would have welcomed working for any Arab country. It was like a mental balancing of the books, correcting the early Beirut dirties through helping an Arab country move forward. Newspapers and magazine people, railway builders and atomic reactor sellers would ask me for help with things Middle Eastern. My friend in Baghdad lived up to his promise and people I sent to Baghdad were facilitated through meetings with high officialdom and sophisticated, organized introductions to "where the future is".

My trips to Baghdad were frequent and high-powered, always involving a companion, an army captain or lieutenant to drive me around, to get me to appointments on time and show me the sights when I wasn't working. There was a constant stream of luncheon and dinner parties and endless friendly meetings with pompous

Foreign Ministry types, television and radio pseudo-hip guys, Ministry of Defense mystery people and ultimately the important people without portfolio, the shadowy people connected with the President's office, the ones whose importance was judged less by title and more by how much they frightened others. I kept moving up the scale. I worked with the Ministry of Defense openly. Dealt with Dr. Najid, the Minister of Information and Adram Harmadi, the important Minister of Planning, who took me under his wing. Most importantly, I developed a special relationship with Barazan Hussein, Head of National Security and brother and chief adviser to the President, titles which gave him license to involve himself in everything.

It was interesting, stimulating and lucrative work. I was doing something I enjoyed which satisfied both sides of me, the Arab half and the American half.

Baghdad was fun in a different way; it oozed glory. Hundreds of mosques with elaborate mosaics reflecting an affinity with deep blue colors. Museums with more Assyrian, Arcadian and Nusterian pieces of art than they could accommodate and Islamic museums bare of anything decorative but full of ancient manuscripts and beautifully bound copies of the Koran that went back hundreds of years, some even a thousand.

The streets were a mixture of the old and new, London-style double-decker buses stopping dead to allow beasts of burden to cross the street. Noisy, narrow, unpaved streets where the smell of meat and spice was choking and noisier eight lane modern highways within a stone's throw of them. And there were the statues extolling the virtues of the farmer and worker with inscriptions in praise of both.

Baghdad had its special air. Things were happening, oil wealth touched every corner of everyday life, but then, unlike Saudi Arabia and Kuwait, you had the unmistakable feeling that the average man was an aware participant in what made the place. It was a lovely city that hugged the Tigris on both sides, even the occasional sandstorm confirmed the place's identity and reminded me of where I was. It was, I guess is, a proud city which could not but touch the hearts and minds of believers in Arab dreams.

My one regret about Baghdad was that the Iraqis' attitude precluded taking Maggie there. She would have enjoyed seeing the ancient books and Arab calligraphy, two of her loves, but the Iraqis expected me to be an Arab, to leave my woman behind. But soon, this almost perfect picture of an organized, purposeful life was being threatened. Iraq's attack on Iran in September 1980 and the ensuing war left me full of jitters. Then, out of the blue, there was Jimmy Darrells, my boss from Beirut days, staying at London's Dorchester Hotel and telephoning to invite me for a drink. His telephone call made me believe the United States viewed the protracted war very seriously indeed.

According to Darrells, he had seen an old friend, Cape Miller, who told him that I was alive and doing exceptionally well and he wanted to meet with me and catch up with things, "to see how the so-and-so is doing". He sounded relaxed and natural, but I knew him well enough to know that the telephone call wasn't an accident.

The Darrells of this world don't make contact by accident; they create and manipulate their universe. They are always in command, working with the precision of a mathematical formula. If Darrells wanted to see me for the first time in over ten years, then there was a reason for it, a good Iraqi reason for it.

The lobby at the Dorchester Hotel at 6:00 p.m. always looks the same: the waiters are full of pompous condescension and the guests effect a relaxed, I-belong-here manner nervously. The furniture, even though it had just been changed, looked the same, unappealing, functional art deco. And Darrells, sitting right across from the revolving door, looked the same. The hair had thinned a tiny bit, but the waist was still trim. The jacket of his suit was a bit too long, but the manner, the firm handshake, the look straight into the eyes and the pat on the shoulder were the same as well. So was the damn jargon.

"Well, we keep an eye on our boys you know!"

"Someone from Beirut days?"

"Yes. I told you, Cape." And a waiter rushed as Darrells raised his hands to clap them.

He was still the boss—in charge from the moment I walked in. To my distress, that included me as well as waiters. It was if nothing had happened. All the years in between seemed to burst like a bubble between Darrells' clapped hands. Only one thing stood between us and kept him from ordering me around the way he did fourteen years ago—her. Maggie appeared in full size. She stood between us. Mentally I had reached for her, and she was there. She didn't let me down, she appeared when I needed her, disapproving.

Yes it all began to make sense and I felt besieged. To hell with the tea and the sweets, with the Dorchester, to hell with Darrells, to hell with everything. Where was she? I wanted her in person, not just a helpful image. I almost screamed for her, wanted to touch her, to ask her help, to wrap my arms around her and declare that she was mine and obliged to save me. But I didn't do any of that. I was playing the game just the way Darrells wanted it—even when he set me up to ask him what he was doing.

"Don't tell me you haven't heard that I am with The Weekly Inquirer *now."*

"I guess I did," I lied.

"Beats the hell out of the Washington Banner *which is no more. I head a special team at WI. We've interviewed Gandhi, Mobutu, Sadat. Come to think of it, your boy, Saddam, is top of the list now. Would love to do him, but they're a pain in the neck—they're demanding a cover story. We'd do them a world of good, if they'd stop all that nonsense. Hell, why don't you talk to them?"*

Darrells was smiling at me the same way he had smiled at Sarkisian.

I told Darrells I would see what I could do and he gave me his direct telephone number in New York. He was leaving the following morning.

My hand was getting tired and so I stopped the letter writing charade and looked out of the window instead. The remembrance of how Darrells came back into my life continued. I couldn't stop that. I didn't even want to.

I had walked the three blocks from the Dorchester to South

Audley Street contemplating my next move. Darrells' *Weekly Inquirer* magazine job was the flimsiest cover I had ever heard of. Should I just ignore him? I couldn't do that, particularly if he had ways of reaching the Iraqis directly, or via different channels. Was he asking me in again? Well he didn't, and the answer to that can wait. What would the Iraqis say, would they have heard about his background and would it incriminate me? Did he have a special message for Saddam Hussein? After all, the US and Iraq hadn't had diplomatic relations since the 1967 War. Surely there were better ways of reaching the Iraqis than through me. There was more to it than what appeared on the surface, that was for damn sure and the Cape Miller nonsense ... that's what it was, nonsense. Cape was the type of old CIA whore Darrells liked because he was weak and easy to manipulate.

By the time I had reached home, I had decided to tell Margaret. She was always Margaret when things were serious. She would be there preparing dinner, chops or something equally simple to suit her anti-cooking sentiments.

I was right—she was in the kitchen. We kissed as always and because I was trying to unload, I told her about Darrells without any preliminaries. I had mentioned him before in the context of Radio Freedom without the damaging details about Sarkisian or the Palestinians. Maggie faced the stove and played with whatever she was cooking, but I could tell she was far from pleased. She had her back turned to me in an unnatural way.

"What's the matter darling? I can't tell him to vanish. I worked with the guy for years."

My attempts to speak of Darrells as an old friend failed. Her voice was menacing.

"What does he want?"

"Don't know really. Perhaps it's just what he says, an interview." I was trying to avoid a confrontation.

"Daoud, do they want you back?"

"Hey, hey," and I tried to put spark in my voice, "I doubt it. I'm out of touch."

Suddenly she acquired the stare of someone who refused to be subdued. "No, you're not. You're close to Iraq and you know it and they know it. In fact, every time you speak about the people of Baghdad and what you're doing, I suspect something's going on already."

"I promise you, nothing is going on and a year ago I promised you nothing would—though you are right. I'm in a special position. There is no way I want any part of Darrells and Co. It's all over, a part of history. Besides, I was with the amateur bunch—Radio Freedom. But he does put me on the spot with his odd request."

My appeals and disclaimers got nowhere. Over dinner, Maggie made me promise her not to get involved again. She complained about the CIA running the world, compared the Americans to boy scouts and made it clear that she was happy with what we had. She described us as lovers and friends in a nice, uncomplicated way.

I remember saying, "Why don't you marry me? Aren't girls the ones who put the pressure on, usually?"

Suddenly she became a little sad, weary. "My parents won't stand for it. No, they don't think Arabs have tails, though they are provincial. They think you're after my money. Are you?"

"What money? I don't know anything about any worthwhile money. Nothing to worry about as far as I know. But obviously you have been discussing the whole thing with them. So why not with me?" Acting hurt was easy because I was hurt.

"What do you want to know? You're slow sometimes. They have money—some of the wealthiest people in England, in the world. All of it comes from my grandmother. She inherited Donge and Honne, the grain concern headquartered in Argentina, the largest privately-owned company in the world. I think they employ over 200,000 people worldwide. I don't know much about it, but money they have."

Maggie had felt a need for relief and was feeling better, while my eyes were popping out with surprise.

"Jesus! I know D and H. Why didn't you ever tell me?" My astonishment was genuine.

"Why? What difference would it make?"

"Nothing really, but it's as if you have been keeping things from me."

"Does it matter if I have money or not?"

"Not to me, though obviously to your parents. I just feel uneasy around this type of money. No wonder your parents—I am—it's odd. I'm not very big on people's parents, but it explains a lot. Are they aware I am a peasant from outside Jerusalem? Do they really know?"

"Listen you, don't go off and act the sensitive bit. I wouldn't let go of you for all the old tombs in Bethany."

"And I wouldn't let go of you even if South America ran out of wheat. You must have been suffering a lot of pressure from them. What an idiot I am."

We reached across to each other and held hands, clasped all four hands together and we were there alone as usual, but happy. God, so very happy and content with what we had and what we were. After the dishes were cleaned we went to bed and made love. It was great and we woke up refreshed and relaxed and made little apologies to each other, promising never to argue again. Maggie followed routine and left at the usual time. Nothing more was said about money or about her parents, but she did look relieved. My friend, my Maggie, had been fighting for me in secret, probably suffering in secret. Oh, God I loved her.

The following morning, I telephoned the Iraqi Press Counselor, and told him I must meet him immediately; it was like a summons. My rising star in Baghdad determined his response and he came to South Audley Street.

Raab Gazzaz loved cigars as much as Darrells did, but he was much smaller, short with the usual Arab paunch, thinning curly black hair and a smiling round face which made the big nose and mustache look like implants. His lighter complexion betrayed a drop of Kurdish or Turkish blood in his background. Middle East embraces were exchanged with too long a pumping of the hand. He sat on the sofa next to my desk, all attention, his feet barely touching the ground.

Darrells' position with *The Weekly Inquirer* was explained and the importance of the publication was mentioned. The possibility of the interview making a cover story was there, but Darrells couldn't guarantee it—other news during the week of the interview would determine that. I explained that Darrells had promised the content of the article would be positive, aimed at improving the atmosphere between Iraq and the US, but couldn't promise more. Darrells was available to go to Baghdad at any time.

Gazzaz was pleased. "A cover story on *The Weekly Inquirer*, wow! We can use that, believe me, Brother Daoud, we can use that. You should talk to his Excellency personally, though. After all," continued a smiling coquettish Gazzaz, "His Excellency, Dr. Najid is your friend." Gazzaz described how he would have to go through elaborate channels to reach the Minister of Information and I agreed. I thanked him for visiting me and sharing his thoughts, though I knew that he would claim some of the credit if the project was a success. After all, the Arabs are the people who kill you and cry at your funeral, or so the saying goes.

CHAPTER NINE

I couldn't possibly put it all in a letter, particularly one I probably wouldn't post, and besides when my hand gets tired the scribbles become unintelligible. For now, the longest letter in history has to be done mentally. Then I will edit it and decide what goes to Anna, if anything.

Dr. Najid answered his direct line with a longer than usual brotherly greeting. Of course Gazzaz hadn't told him. After all, he was available to me at all times and there was no need for Gazzaz. *The Weekly Inquirer,* it's the biggest. Why can't Darrells guarantee a cover story? Yes, it was important. They knew about Darrells, he was a big man. The type the Brother President would talk to. The idea was good, but no firm date could be fixed. Could Darrells come to Baghdad and wait a day or two? After all, there was a war on and the President, the hero leader, was at the front with his "soldier brothers" most of the time. I told Najid I'd be back to him the following day.

In the afternoon I telephoned Darrells, "You're on, provided you don't insist on a fixed day. Saddam is playing General most of the time and has to fit you in between trips to the front. A wait of a day or two perhaps."

"Understand. How about in two weeks? I'll take Sam Dreles with me. He's Greek-American and pro-Arab and knows the area. He's done some pieces which were favorable to them."

"Dreles is okay. I'll be back to you tomorrow about the date."

"Listen, thanks. This is good of you, but then you're one of us. Many thanks indeed."

"No problem."

The next day, by the time I telephoned Najid, then Darrells, it was all arranged. For security reasons, Darrells and Dreles were to pick up their visas at the Iraqi Embassy in Amman and proceed to Baghdad from there. Christ, I thought to myself, here by the grace of Darrells go I again.

I had to tell Maggie. I just had to. So I did it that evening when we were in Daphne's restaurant, the same place I took her the first time we went out.

"Maggie, Darrells is going to Baghdad. I arranged it. If he gets Saddam Hussein on the cover of *The Weekly Inquirer*, then the sky is the limit. They'll do anything for me."

I had never seen her look so hurt. "You couldn't help it. Why? Just tell me why! For money? We don't need money."

"I had to do it. Darrells would have gone directly and I'd have been blamed for not transmitting a message." My hushed tone suggested that she should keep her voice down.

"Don't say that. Give me the big picture. Why? Ever since that bastard appeared—ever since three days ago—you have been a different person. You talk about him as if he were God. You're afraid of him. You want to be close to him. Do you want to go back to them? Honestly?"

"No."

"Honestly, I said." She stared at me.

"Yes and no." It was a feeble answer delivered feebly.

"Why the 'yes'?"

"Because Iraq needs help. I am an Arab. If I can help them, then I will."

"You've got to tell me more than that."

So I had a quick look around the place while deciding what to say. "Well, people around us are into their food so I will. I really do want to help Iraq, but I can't directly. I'm a half-breed, neither Arab nor American. I love both, but can't openly go beyond a certain point with either. If I can't help directly, then why not indirectly by getting them together?"

"There's more to it. Deep there in you, what is it?" It was a combination of a plea and a condemnation.

"Power. It's a spiritual uplift. To hell with inducing Dechtel to go back to Iraq to build pipelines. To hell with finding them British companies to extend credit. To hell with planting the occasional story on their behalf. Maggie, if what I suspect is true, if Darrells is going to talk to Saddam in the name of the President of the US, then that is something else." I attached a look of defiance to my statement, hoping to make it sound believable, to overwhelm her protests.

"You really become arrogant just talking about it. There's an unattractive smirk which shows—you can't even hide it." She shook her head in a gesture of exasperation.

There was nothing to do except continue in the same vein. "Maggie, Maggie, my love. Why should I be confined to making money, to trading? A bit of history, even through the back door would be satisfying—for me. You, you don't know how it feels to be in the middle. We cultural half-breeds can't be heroes to either side. We can't be accepted by people like your parents. We remain novelties, oddities all our lives. I don't have a Wiltshire to go to when London gets on my nerves; I don't have a Bethany any more. I am nowhere." Because I meant it, I thought that it would work, but it didn't.

"Isn't what we have enough? You know I think it's a dirty business, spying. What's wrong with trading? Am I not enough? Why not quit? We'll go settle in the South of France. You like it there."

There was no going back, so I decided to go all the way. "Oh, Maggie, it isn't that simple. Don't say you aren't enough—you should know better. You're right about the magazine bit, though. In spite of the wonders of America, I always thought I would end up in the Middle East doing something worthwhile, perhaps teaching. Radio Freedom took care of that. Even though others didn't know it, the stint with Radio Freedom forced me into total Americana. Hells bells, I was not enough of a cynic to pretend otherwise. Every time an old classmate from Beirut days made it to the top, I used to have visions of one of them remembering me and sending for me to do something important, to help him. If nothing else, I thought that they would remember that a Chinese boy by the name of Lee Mansing and I achieved the highest scholastic record in the history of the American University of Beirut. I was a star athlete, tennis and soccer. I was head of the student council. I was years ahead of the crowd and I actually thought someone would remember and send for me. Okay, the Iraqis did, to do a side job. After the Radio Freedom mess that's as far as it will go, but I like it. I'm after what belongs to me—my little place in the Middle East sun, not money. The answer to your question is yes and no—really. I need to do something Arab and it appears that cooperating with the Americans is necessary to do it. It beats going through life celebrating success through collecting Hermes ties and going to good restaurants.

"How I see things now is not easy to explain. To you, Khomeini is an intellectual exercise, a news item, a bad guy whom you see from far away and you relate to what he does more than you relate to what he is. To me it's more serious. He challenges hundreds of years of tradition. Everything the Moslem and Arab worlds ever stood for is being tested. Our whole being is on the front line and if people don't oppose him, then they are his accomplices. I am in a unique position to damage him, and you're right, I am arrogant enough to believe that. The chance to recapture part of my dream by standing up to the monster is here. I need it for me and because it's right. You may think I'm crazy, but I'm after him. The boy scout brigade, Darrells, is giving me that chance."

There was no drama in what followed, just a matter of fact correction that was meant to hurt and humiliate. "They're not going to send for you, that's for sure. Nobody will send for you. And as far as I am concerned it will always be a dirty business and the talk about the back door to history is utter nonsense. But you want it, it's part of your makeup. It's the meddling which appeals, not the pure purpose. It was there before I was there, the itch to be involved. Surely you can oppose Khomeini openly without all this messiness. You misled me, made me believe it was over. How very, very unfair. If you only knew what you mean to me . . . how difficult my family has been."

"Maggie, you're more important to me than anything else in the world, you know that. Listen, you are not going to cry. Let's go home. Come on . . . let's go."

I took her home and we didn't say a word to each other all the way. We just went to bed. Before we fell asleep, I managed to get hold of her hand and squeeze it. I didn't know what to say and she had decided against further discussion. The squeeze back was very light indeed. What a criminal thing to do, to show her that she didn't understand, that in spite of her commitment to me she wasn't enough to keep me happy. God only knows what her family had put her through. It hasn't been easy for her and I . . . I just can't help it. I don't think it's meddling. After all, they came after me. I am the perfect man for this job. A chance meeting with history . . . no, no, not meddling.

I was getting closer to the heart of the matter. I am over the part with Maggie that should hurt, but it still does. I still think I was right. Women don't understand these things . . . don't know why, but they don't. Perhaps women don't dream the way men do, I don't know. Do women dream? Anna, Caroline, Betsy, Diana, Jean, Marianne, Sarah . . . all of you out there, tell me that women don't dream. It would make life easier . . . tell me.

CHAPTER TEN

Thinking about the letter to Anna took hours, most of the flight time to Washington. It served several purposes including avoiding any thoughts about Brandt and what to tell him. My subconscious made the proposed letter untidy; the more I wanted to write about Maggie, the more Darrells got in the way. Yes—Darrells was always in the way, though I hoped Brandt would live up to his promise and not include him in this meeting. He had initiated the Iraqi affair, but Dr. Raji was different. Dr. Raji was mine.

Darrells had done a good job for Iraq. He put Saddam Hussein on the cover of *The Weekly Inquirer*, grim in a military uniform without rank or insignia, showing his toughness through a deliberate frown. Inside, in the publisher's letter, was a picture of Darrells and Dreles with Saddam and a brief description of how they had spent seven hours with him after waiting two days to do the interview. The question and answer part had lasted three hours and then Saddam, annoyed because one of their questions suggested he wasn't popular, had taken them on a tour of Baghdad in his armor-plated car with about fifteen other cars full of security people in hot pursuit. *The Weekly Inquirer* said Saddam was popular; they even descended into everyday jargon and described him as charismatic and said that the crowds in the streets of Baghdad loved him. Reading between the lines, I decided that the whole exercise was aimed at better US–Iraqi relations. Saddam had hinted at the opening, "The moment American spare parts stop reaching Iran and we see indications of an even-handed policy between the Arabs and Israel, then we will be ready to restore diplomatic relations with the US."

It was too good to be true, Darrells acting as a mouthpiece for the Iraqi regime. Gazzaz had telephoned to congratulate me and said fifty copies of the WI were being shipped via diplomatic bag to Baghdad so that everyone would see the results of my "grand work". Two days later, Dr. Najid telephoned to thank me, announcing with undisguised Arab pride that a little present from the President was on its way to me. Iraqi happiness was confirmed by the President's brother. Barazan called to repeat Dr. Najid's message and to invite me to Baghdad to meet himself.

Everyone in Iraq behaved as if I had written the WI story myself. I didn't mind. I had been looking forward to a trip to Baghdad and a week of hugs and embraces. That, however, was delayed by a message from Dr. Najid who, in a totally Arab turn around, was in a deep funk. The US Government was refusing to allow the American Aircraft Company to sell additional jumbo jets, 323 civilian planes to Iraq. "It doesn't make sense," he had shouted. Wasn't our friend Darrells the US Government? Why was the US always behaving in a contradictory fashion? I must contact Darrells and do something about this, perhaps go to see him. Darrells, their new-found friend, must fix it. My response was vague except to satisfy his Arab ego by calling the whole episode a huge mistake.

Deeper and deeper . . . where the hell was Darrells? New York had claimed he was in Amman on his way back via London, but Dr. Najid's request couldn't wait. After considerable effort, I found him at the International Hotel in Amman writing his interview with King Hussein. It sounded as if he was attempting to resurrect the image of an overlooked monarch. I didn't give him much of a chance to thank me. I went into Dr. Najid's problem right away. He took it calmly and asked me to call Dr. Najid and assure him that all would be well in two days.

I had difficulty in relaying the message to Dr. Najid. As occasionally happened, Baghdad was unobtainable by telephone for two days and by the time I reached Najid on the third day, *The Wall Street Financier* carried a lead story urging the US Government to sell the 323s to Iraq. It described the refusal to grant an export license as "counter-productive". Lo and behold, the State Department, as if awaiting a signal, announced through a spokesman that an export license would be granted. Iraq, the State Department claimed without going into details, no longer supported terrorism and therefore the US Government would withdraw its objection to the sale of the 323s.

Dr. Najid was ecstatic. "Come to Baghdad," he had said on the phone, "the Brother President is anxious to see you. Come any time soon. The Press Counselor will arrange your visa and ticket. Call him right away. Also, please don't forget to thank our very dear friend Mr. Darrells."

My unexpected change of fortune found me shaking my head and smiling like an absentminded alcoholic. Calling Gazzaz and telling him I was Baghdad-bound was easier than telling Maggie. But then I had to tell her. There was no way out.

I took her to the theater to see the play *Good*. The plot had parts which fed into our unfinished argument. It was a portrayal of a simple ordinary German who turns into a Nazi monster because he is swept away by the atmosphere of power which claims and then corrupts him. Later when we went for an after-theater dinner, we talked about the play and how good the acting was. I could tell Maggie wanted to say more about it, but didn't want to restart our argument. I wished to God that telling her about going to Baghdad wasn't necessary, but it was.

"Maggie, I'm off to Baghdad in a day or two. Soon as Darrells is back and I see him."

"I guessed you would. I saw the cover story. Well done—just what the doctor ordered. Not a word about all of the innocent Iraqis who disappear in the middle of the night just because they disagree with Saddam. How many people has he executed so far?" This time there was an angry shrillness in her voice.

"God damn it! He's still better than the other side and that's what's important. He can be got rid of in time, unlike the Khomeini movement. What the hell is the matter? That's the way the world works, opting for lesser evils."

"The world is what we make it, and you have chosen your way. It's none of my business. Just don't shout at me, here or anywhere else."

I tried to control my rising anger. "Maggie, won't you understand? The President wants to see me. In the middle of a war and a million other things, he wants to see *me*. He has something he wants to tell me."

"Then go to see him. I knew you would go for it. It's your life."

"What the hell is this?" Then I recovered and tried to hold her hand and pet it while I looked at the table.

"It's nothing. Go and satisfy your ego. You won't be happy any other way. Your craving for power comes first."

I did what people in corners do, I tried to saddle her with the decision. "Listen my love, if you don't want me to go, then I won't go."

"Go. That's what you want to do. It's what you need. If I stopped you, you'd never forgive me . . . and you promised."

A heavy silence descended upon us. This was new. She was pulling away, a wall was being erected between us. It wasn't a quarrel—it was something bigger. A huge divide separated us, a distance, a sudden absence of the ability to communicate. Even looking into her eyes didn't work. That light within was gone, extinguished. Could it be that her support for Save the Whale groups was genuine? Would she really be happier in jeans taking care of me in a little shack in the South of France? Perhaps what she claimed was right, that she loved me because I had an air of human need about me, a longing which showed on my face and she had thought it was for love, for her. Perhaps, just perhaps, I didn't know her.

There was nothing to do except pay the bill and go home, a silent unhappy journey with both of us looking out of the taxi window to avoid looking at each other and more hurtful exchanges. I went into the bedroom and to bed while she characteristically attended to the cat box. I was still awake when she came in, undressed and went to bed. My attempt at holding her hand failed. I got my hand patted in acknowledgment, a long way from making love just by looking at each other. Eventually we fell into uneasy sleep, but the remoteness was still there the following morning when she left unusually early after planting a cold perfunctory kiss on my forehead. Something went with her.

The air ticket came from the Iraqi Embassy with a note about a diplomatic car taking me to the airport. The same afternoon Maggie called to tell me she was tired and was staying home. She reminded me to attend to the cat's food and box. At 7:00 p.m. the telephone rang and Darrells invited me to join him at The Dorchester, if I was free. He had just arrived and I was free and didn't want to think about what Maggie's telephone call meant.

I was with Darrells by 7:30 p.m. He was a new, improved Darrells with a smile broader than anything I'd ever seen. We settled to have a drink at The Dorchester bar and he couldn't wait to regale me with the details of his trip.

"Saddam is no socialist, God damn it. I guess it was fashionable to be a socialist when he was young, but his instincts are capitalist. Iraq has got a big story to tell, important to all of us, the whole world. You should do something about it, Daoud. If they don't use people like you, then hell, they can't do anything right. However, the door is wide open and the story in the magazine should make life easier for you. Lets face it, I couldn't say more without sounding like one of his house organs."

The elevation, enticement and open invitation to cooperate didn't escape me, but I was much more concerned with making a point. "Jimmy, what about *The Wall Street Financier*? How did you do that?"

"Well, there are always ways. The request was timely. You did me and the Iraqis a great service. As I said, the whole thing was timely." And this time he pretended to wink like an Arab. For a second I wanted to hit him. I really had an urge to grab him off the stool and do it, but I settled for something considerably less. "Jimmy, I don't want to front for anyone. If it is the same old game, then I must have a say about what is done and how. I'm a free agent now. I want to stay free."

"There is no old game, no new game. I know Washington well, you know that. There are ways of doing this sort of thing. You got what you asked for and now you're complaining." As usual, he guessed my mood and played it the right way.

"I'm not complaining. I just want to know. I am quite happy to help both sides, but I don't want to be used. I don't know where this whole thing is going!" The despair showed, and with it an utter helplessness.

"Not a chance, my boy. Why should you be used? They should get together, Iraq and the US. But stay in touch and I'll do the same. I'm sorry we can't have dinner. I'm eating with Lord Mancy, knew him years ago when I came to the London School of Economics after Yale."

"I didn't know you went to LSE."

"Oh yes—two years here. Just after the war, just when things went wrong with the Russians."

Darrells couldn't help his abruptness, the inherent bitchiness which commanded him to reassert himself, to reestablish the true level of our relationship. Why not? He knew the Iraqis would want me to stay in touch with him. He knew me well enough to know that I loathed Khomeini, that working against him was what my ego and the ruins of my ideology needed. As a matter of fact, he knew that I would never pull out.

The following day I tried to reach Maggie by phone a number of
times, but there was no answer, just the answerphone. I left a
message reminding her of my departure time and said something
about the cats.

Gazzaz came with me to the airport. Iraqi Airways afforded me
VIP treatment and Gazzaz himself, full of smiles and the smell of
cigars, came aboard the plane to emphasize my importance to the
cabin staff. The plane took off at 4:00 p.m. London time so that it
might arrive in Baghdad at night to avoid possible Iranian war
planes.

My companion was waiting, an over-six-foot first lieutenant who
identified me, clicked his heels in respect and handed my passport
to someone to stamp it and bring it to me later at the hotel. He
ushered me into a car parked in front of the airport building. The
car's parking spot was quite a feat reflecting favorably on my
importance; the Iraqis didn't allow cars within half a mile of the
terminal building for fear of bombs placed by dissidents or
saboteurs sent in by Iran.

At the hotel, all I had to do was sign a guest card already
prepared for me. My companion was under orders to pick me up
at 10:00 a.m. the following morning.

The first thing I did was to place a call to Maggie. She was there.

"I just got in. Sorry I missed you earlier today."

"I was out." I decided not to react to the challenging tone of the
answer.

"How are you?"

"I'm alright. How is romantic Baghdad? Are you getting your
VIP treatment?" The edge was still there.

"Haven't seen much of it yet. Just got into my fancy suite."

"Give my regards to the goons!"

"Maggie, please, have you gone crazy?" I stopped myself before
any mention of telephone taps.

"A little bit. Anyway, get some pistachio nuts if your busy
schedule permits, the way you used to."

"I will. Anything else?" It was an attempt at being playful.

"No. Just come back in one piece. Don't go floating in the Tigris
against your will."

"I'll be back. Four days, you'll see. Give my love to the cats."

Sleep was easy in spite of Maggie's barbs; I had got what I
wanted to hear.

At exactly 10:00 a.m., there was a knock on the door. My tall companion clicked his heels and announced that we were going to see Dr. Najid and Brother Barazan Hussein at the Ministry of Information, a few miles out of town.

My companion pointed out everything along the way, be it old or new, a mosque yards away from a new power station, a luxury power boat with a shining huge instrument panel piloted by someone with a native headdress and baggy Western trousers. Smart, aggressive-looking members of the Special Forces were mentioned with particular pride, but there was not a word about the war atmosphere, the sandbags and barbed wire around the buildings, the anti-aircraft guns everywhere, that peculiar weariness in the faces of a people at war, the blankness which repressed the natural gleam and concealed the native vitality of most Iraqis. The wartime blackout had reached the people; there was a dimness of heart in the streets of Baghdad.

At the end of the road was the tall, modern building surrounded by greenery and what looked like an endless number of iron gates manned by sentries with machine guns at the ready. On top of it was what looked like a whole anti-aircraft battery. The guards stopped us at each of the three iron gates, but let us through without a search. Except for the unnatural extras, the building could have been in London, Paris or Munich; its only concession to location were the murals depicting the usual glorification of Iraqi workers and farmers looking healthy and happy. Allah, a word which adorns public buildings in other Middle East countries, was conspicuously absent.

The lift took us to the third floor where my companion surrendered me to a ministerial aide and returned downstairs to wait. My new mentor led the way and there was a gentle knock on a wooden door, Dr. Najid's office, and the door opened to two outstretched arms which wrapped themselves around me in a close hug while Dr. Najid kissed me incessantly, moving from one cheek to the other. In between them was the deep "Welcome, welcome, welcome home."

Dr. Najid let go of me, then it was Barazan's turn. Tall and bearded, he was a little less dramatic, but he did kiss me four times, repeating the welcome and, out of character, had a big broad smile on his face.

I sat down on the large sofa where Dr. Najid indicated he

wanted me, right next to him. Barazan Hussein was across the room in a deep, cushioned chair. Except for the mandatory picture of Saddam it was the office of a middle rank executive. Dr. Najid, rubbing himself with undisguised joy, started. "How are you?"

"I am very well, very well indeed and pleased to be here."

"We hope you are," and he eyed Barazan to confirm that the latter shared his sentiment. "Baghdad is the home of every Arab. We want all our brothers to be comfortable here. Was the flight alright? Is the hotel okay?" Insistent hospitality was the order of the moment.

"I am in excellent shape. Everything was well organized — couldn't be better — and the brother lieutenant has been showing me around Baghdad. He is extremely nice."

This was interrupted; even nice Dr. Najid didn't seem to give a damn about what they called a brother officer and what followed was the classic Arab promise which is always beyond fullfilment. "When the war is over, the keys to Baghdad will be yours. Everything has an end, even this war. But now is Darrells happy? The President spent seven hours with him! That's a lot of time for the President to spare. You see how much we value your friends."

So it was all for me, hmm. "Darrells is on top of the world."

Barazan was visibly edgy. He wanted to dispense with the niceties so he interrupted the Minister. "As you Americans say, let's get down to business. Tell us more about Darrells, Daoud."

"Well, he is a big man, Editor of *The Weekly Inquirer*, has high level connections in Washington, very high."

"We know that. How close is he to the US Government? Can he influence things?" This particular interruption, undisguised rudeness, was made without a smile.

"He knows who to talk to. He knows his way round Washington. He has been there for years."

Barazan kept pushing, interrupted a third time. "Is he Government or is he just a journalist?"

"I don't think he's Government. I thought he was strictly *Weekly Inquirer*."

"No, no, Dreles is strictly *Weekly Inquirer*. He is still here, kisses everyone he meets in a friendly Greek way. Right now he's reporting a battle in the south, always drunk. He's a lightweight. Darrells is something else. Darrells is important. He wants to help us, he said."

We chuckled until I decided to save the poor Greek. "Forget about Dreles and his drinking. Though he's a very nice chap and we can use him, he does what Darrells tells him. Just a field reporter, but he is still *Weekly Inquirer* so he should be treated well."

Barazan continued. "We are not concerned with Dreles, believe me, but Darrells . . . can he live up to his promises? Can he get us Cobra helicopters or TOW anti-tank missiles?"

"Brother Barazan, I don't know. This is something new. I doubt it. You are asking for the most sophisticated stuff they have. Their misguided policy is to remain neutral—not to supply either side with arms. That is a big order. I don't even know whether Darrells would want to get involved. I just don't know." I sighed. My unease about getting into a boring conversation about Congress and the Jewish lobby showed.

"They don't have to sell to us directly. There are other ways. Through Nigeria, the UAE or someone else who would pretend to buy them and then resell to us. It's all the same to us as long as we get the hardware." Barazan was staring right at me while Dr. Najid had his hands nervously clutched between his knees.

"Forget the UAE. How many of them can they order and still look legitimate? Nigeria maybe. You have to have a country with an army of a certain size to justify placing an order for such sophisticated hardware. I'll try Darrells when I get back to London. There's no harm in asking." I was already thinking of a way out of the predicament.

"No, it can't wait. We have to know fast. Call him from here. Today preferably. The hotel is already treating your telephone calls as top priority. They will make sure you get through."

I nodded agreement and Barazan and I, thinking of my previous telephone calls, smiled at each other, but I decided against trying to explain Maggie.

That over, our talk reverted to London and the number of Arabs who lived there and endless stories of their misbehavior. Barazan and an again relaxed Dr. Najid thought London was nothing but a huge bar—casino—nightclub full of Arabs who paid blondes thousands of pounds for a night of pleasure and drove around the city in pink Rolls Royces. Near noon, Barazan stood up and said, "Well, let's go to eat. There is a boat restaurant owned by an illiterate Lebanese newspaperman. He's a thief, but he has an

Armenian chef and the fish is exquisite. There is no fish like our *masgoof* in the whole world."

"All Lebanese journalists are illiterate, but I am glad this one has a good cook."

We chuckled and went off in Barazan's car with him at the wheel. Dr. Najid was insistent on sitting in the back seat while I joined Barazan in the front. There was a black car in front and one behind, both full of plainclothes security men, the typical badly dressed, swarthy types always with a thick mustache and a bulge on the side. Cars moved out of Barazan's way as if his car were an ambulance. Then suddenly Dr. Najid smiled at me and whispered something in Barazan's ear, but he decided against keeping it a secret and shouted to no one in particular, "He was a son of a dog while he was alive and he is still a son of a dog." Then eyeing me sideways, he decided to respond to my implicit curiosity. "We have to avoid Freedom Square. There has been a hanging there—the former Minister of Health. He bought bad medicine which caused many deaths in the army, so the President made him pay the price. He is hanging in Freedom Square, a lesson for all those who want to cheat the people." The combination of the news and the Baghdad dust seeping through the slightly open window forced me into a dry cough, but I said nothing. It is hard to be down and out in a dictatorship, a revered excellency a week ago, a traitor now and the regime's rabble rousers gathering the faithful in Freedom Square to jeer at a lifeless body.

When Barazan almost ran over an innocent pedestrian, I wondered how many official cars were recognized by the Baghdad populace, how many times a day the speeding black symbols of authority reminded people of what kind of government they had. This haughty behavior is peculiar to Barazan and the President's family, I thought. Look at the way he treats poor Najid.

What would Maggie say about Iraqi justice—the fact that there probably was no trial? What would Barazan say to me if I queried him about all this, about the man's qualifications as a "filthy son of a dog"?

Yes, it was a very pleasantly decorated riverboat, an obvious attempt at imitating boat restaurants everywhere, even with an overabundance of marine memorabilia and old maps. Obviously we were expected; the staff in black trousers and white jackets were waiting for us, standing at attention. The head waiter bowed and led us to a corner table which was already covered by about thirty plates of appetizers, from crushed chick peas in sesame butter to grilled chicken wings in lemon sauce. There was no one else in the place except us, an unsurprising security precaution which also meant the Lebanese journalist's restaurant was used for official entertaining. Maybe his illiteracy endeared him to the people in power.

I sat between Dr. Najid and Barazan and we resumed our conversation about Darrells as if nothing had intervened. They told me the President liked him, but they were not sure whether they could trust him. They wanted to use him as a channel to the US. As there had been no diplomatic relations between the two countries since 1967, they had been using King Hussein of Jordan to transmit messages to the US. That was no good—Jordan's outlook was different and they feared the messages were being doctored somewhere along the way. They didn't trust King Hussein all that much and wondered whether the Americans did.

We returned to the point we'd left hanging earlier—Darrells, who he was, how big, how far he could be trusted. Our talk never strayed far from those themes, and the more they talked the more the problem became clear to me. Either I distance myself from Darrells or I build him up and encourage them to make more use of him and risk being suspected of working for the US myself. Should I put an end to that? No. Hell, I wouldn't do that. The number one government in the Middle East was asking me for help and I enjoyed it. Darrells would love it. Perhaps he expected it. So much achieved in a few hours. I reconfirmed to them I would ask Darrells about helicopters and missiles when I spoke to him, hopefully later that day. They reemphasized the need for a speedy answer.

That done, I decided the time had come to discuss the reason for my presence.

"When will I be presented to the Brother President? You don't know how much I look forward to this honor." I tried to wear my best look of happiness.

Barazan patted my hand reassuringly. "Tomorrow. Stay on call. Don't leave the hotel. We will tell you when we see you tonight. We're taking you to Khan Marjan, the old caravanserai converted into a club. Arabic folk music like you have never heard. But first make sure that you speak to Darrells. We'll pick you up later."

He made his priorities abundantly clear.

The appetizers and the delicious grilled fish with local beer made me sleepy. At about 3:00 p.m., I was driven back in a special car, while Dr Najid and Barazan stayed behind. The moment I got into the hotel I placed a call to Darrells in New York. When I couldn't find him in New York, I asked the hotel operator to try his Washington number, uncomfortably aware that it was 7:00 a.m. eastern seaboard time. This time I was lucky.

"Jimmy, Daoud. Sorry about the hour, but I'm calling from Baghdad." I was as agreeable as the circumstances allowed.

"Good. Are all of our friends happy?"

"Yes, they are. They like you, but then they don't know you." There was a proper chuckle.

"Right. What can I do for you?"

"Listen, I'm not sure this is the best way to discuss this, but they need some hardware and they would like us to arrange it. I don't think it can wait."

"Speak out. What is it that they want?"

"Well, TOW missiles and Cobra helicopters equipped with the missiles too. Indirectly if not directly, maybe through Nigeria or the Sudan."

"Christ Almighty! Who told you that?" There actually was a change in his voice.

"Barazan and Dr. Najid. It's a very serious request from the top. They don't want to make the request through Jordan, but through us. Don't trust King Hussein for a lot of reasons including his sidekicks' commission levels. His family and friends are charging them thirty percent commission on some hardware. Someone's got to talk to this guy. He's being nasty to our friends."

There was a pause, then Darrells answered. "Listen, forget about Hussein for now. Give me a day or two. A day. This has to go all the way up to National Security Council. Some of our own units need TOW. It won't be easy. I will try to call you later tonight. Don't make any promises. It's a toughie, but if anyone can do it then it's the National Security boys—not State."

"Okay."

"We'll see what can be done, talk later."

I took a nap, got up and called Maggie, but she wasn't there. Where was she? I needed to speak to her, to hear her voice, to obtain reassurance, to maintain the link to the real world, but she wasn't there. Telephonic communications are a bad way of mending things, of retrieving what has been lost through hurt, but I wanted to try. I had to try.

Khan Marjan is a place which starts late and I was waiting to be picked up when the phone rang.

"Daoud, Jimmy. The answer is no. I couldn't even get an intelligent conversation started on the subject. Congress and the Israeli lobby would raise hell. The NSC boys are in bed with Begin. The whole thing is completely out of the question. But listen, we're willing to help them get similar stuff from Britain."

"They want US gear. They were very specific," I moaned.

"Well, Christ, what for? The Westland Lynx helicopter is as good as the Cobra if properly equipped, and they can get something like the TOW."

It was time for a sales pitch. "I think this will disappoint them. They obviously liked you, they trusted you. This was the test and the whole damn thing puts me in a real tight spot. I am the bearer of bad news."

"Can't help with this one, just can't do it, but I will see that we do something to reconfirm our friendship. We value it as well." I could hear Darrells thinking.

"A thought, why don't you deal with them directly? If I can't produce, then I want out of this. I don't like my position in the middle. It's time for me to get back to my everyday business."

This time I got told off. "No, you don't. This is much more important than other things. We are very interested in what they want. Tell them the Executive and State are in their favor, it's all the damn people in Congress and the NSC–Begin setup. You must explain that in your own way. Congress will turn around in time. They hate the Ayatollah because of the embassy hostages, but it's too early to help Iraq directly. You know what I'm talking about. I tried to say this to President Saddam, so please explain it to Barazan and Dr. Najid. It's important. And, hey, keep the lines open. This side doesn't like King Hussein as a middleman either. As you said, he's got his own axe to grind."

"Okay, I'll see what I can do. I'll try."

"Try hard, you can do it. They have to appreciate the divisions which exist here."

"Okay."

I was thankful that by the time my telephone conversation with Darrells had finished, my companion was already downstairs waiting. Once again he explained the building along the way to Khan Marjan, and I came near to asking him why the streets were empty, then I remembered that everyone was in the center of town watching the gruesome display of the "government of the people". The former Minister was spending the night in Freedom Square.

Darrells was up to his old manipulations. His plan was beyond me, whatever it was, but I set this aside when we reached Khan Marjan and I saw Barazan and Dr. Najid who were in a dimly lit corner which received a lot of service attention. The Khan was one huge, high-ceilinged square room with low wooden tables surrounded symmetrically with cushioned chairs. The walls were bare, not even displaying Saddam's picture. The entertainment went on nonstop, first a female singer and then a male one, a folk dance group, another male singer and a lot of clapping and shouting from an appreciative audience. The appetizers in front of us were different from the noon ones, a particularly delicious item made from pomegranate seed juice, a natural sweet and sour sauce—more Iraqi than Lebanese this time.

Again Barazan was the one who started the heavy conversation after dispensing with the endless flowery niceties and the brief on the history of the Khan.

"Did you speak to Darrells?"

"Yes, Brother Barazan, the answer to the request is no."

"Why?"

"Congress would not approve it."

"What about President Reagan?"

"He can't do it without congressional approval."

"Isn't he the President?" The question betrayed more unhappiness than anger.

"Him or Nancy, take your pick." And then, remembering where and with whom I was, I tried to retrieve the unfortunate comment. "To sell sophisticated pieces of armament, congressional approval is needed, and Reagan can't get it so they won't even try."

"Who did Darrells speak to?"

"Don't know. I think McClane, the head of the National Security Council, and probably Chicione, the head of the Iraqi desk at the State Department. Perhaps he went higher. I don't know."

"But the US Military Attaché in Amman told one of our people to make the request, that we would get the goods. They have more governments in America than they do in Lebanon. Who do we believe?"

I was pleased with myself. Barazan was pleading, begging. "The Attaché in Amman is speaking through his ass—if you forgive me. I know the US governmental system, and what you want isn't possible, believe me. I wish to Allah I was wrong, but you must believe me. Darrells is nearer the top than toy soldiers solving world problems on the spot."

"The Americans always cheat us. They promise and then renege. They are always doing the same thing." He continued to plead.

"Dr. Najid, explain to Brother Barazan. You know their system. It isn't possible. Some of their army units need TOW. It's the most sophisticated thing they have. But, believe me, Darrells didn't close the door. He wants to help. He said the US would help you get equivalent stuff from Britain like Lynx helicopters ... and a substitute for TOW. He wants to help."

I was trying to control the situation by, in the words of Darrells, keeping the door open.

"Son of a dog, Darrells. We don't want the Lynx. We want the Cobras. They were effective in Vietnam. We know what we want, our military have considered both helicopters and we want the Cobra. If we wanted Lynx, we would get it directly. Britain is broke and would sell anything." Culture intervened and the plea was turned into an accusation of betrayal.

"Well at least Darrells is willing to be used as a channel. It sounds as if the Americans don't want King Hussein for an intermediary either. His relationship with them isn't what it used to be because he's got his own ideas about how things should be and they don't coincide with theirs. They don't want him to speak for them."

The silences between our exchanges were becoming longer and I was trying to make a silk purse out of Darrells' sow's ear offer. To complete his usual trick, I pretended I was doing them a favor.

Dr. Najid changed the subject to Baghdad, to Khan Marjan, to the Arab culture and the plan of his Ministry to enter an Iraqi-made film at the Cannes Film Festival. He also told me my present from the President would be given to me as I left. Dr. Najid was a nice man, a vanishing breed of Arab gentleman. He was also a clever man who was trying to save Barazan from making a mistake. Military uniforms were mandatory for all Ministers because of the war with Iran, but Najid's hung on him totally out of character, and the .45 he sported looked too heavy for his frail body while his gestures betrayed an inherent shyness. Barazan was different. He had a military, aggressive air. Carrying a gun became him—the type who would use it and ask questions later. He was the Arab counterpart of a macho colonel in a banana republic.

I was feeling tired. It took something out of me being constantly on my toes. There was too much drink, too much food and it was late. I really wanted to go back to the hotel and call Maggie. Eventually, after midnight, I managed politely to excuse myself and return to the hotel using the meeting the following morning as an excuse.

For a change my companion was quiet, but then as the car rose off the ground with a heave and I was drained of all blood, he spat out of the open window of the car and announced, "It's an Iranian rocket. They're trying to hit the TV station near your hotel." Then he spat again and produced a practiced, unpleasant grunt of derision. He wanted to say more, but the sounds of the ack-ack guns drowned his words and mine. I had wanted to tell them to save their ammunition and not shoot at imaginary planes because the rocket had already landed—probably in one of the poor quarters of the city. Instead, I breathed a sigh of relief as I entered the suite and lunged for the phone to call Maggie.

"Hello, my love."

"Hello." Neutrally.

"How's wese?"

"I'm fine. How is the cat and mouse game?"

"Maggie, please stop it. I'm tired. Don't argue with me on the phone."

"Am I?"

"Yes, you are."

My attempt at being forceful failed. "Then I am. I want to go to sleep. I don't want to know anything."

"Don't you want to talk to me?"

"Don't have much to say that's new."

"How are the cats?"

"The same."

"Do they miss me more than you do?"

"Yes, they miss you and so do I, you idiot. You stupid idiot. I hope you know what you are doing." Her voice choked.

"I do."

"I hope so."

Wanton abandon took over. "It's for you. Don't you want me to be happy and relaxed with lots of money, an old man who tells tales about the adventures in the good old days?"

"I want you to go to bed because you have been drinking." She sniffed and snickered.

"I will if you tell me you love me."

"No."

"Why not?"

"Because I'm beginning to wonder. I *am* beginning to wonder." And there was nothing on the line except the sound of silence.

"Maggie?"

"Of course I love you. Hurry home. Leave everything behind and hurry home. Don't worry about money and nonsense, just come home, you fool."

"I love you."

"That's nice to hear."

"Anything more?"

"No. . . ." She hung up, crying.

I couldn't sleep. She had always volunteered the I-love-you statement. This time I had had to extract it from her. It wasn't a passing thing and it registered. Maybe she was right. What was this all about? Barazan very Arab, first making aggressive demands, then begging. Darrells' manipulations to protect a newfound position and then Dr. Najid glimpsing my predicament and defusing the situation by talking about the nicer things of life. Maggie would like Dr. Najid, she would appreciate his sensitivity and his manner, the fact that he seemed to embody all the old values she so loved. She would talk to him about the library of old Arabic scripts in Aden. And me in the middle again. The next day would tell how far I had gone. I would be seeing Saddam Hussein himself. I decided I had better go to sleep and I did, just resisting another telephone call to Maggie.

I was up and about at 6:00 a.m., ordered breakfast and the local newspapers. Saddam's pictures were on every front page, just as they were every day. A bit of overkill, I thought to myself. But then he was an impressive looking young man of forty-six, a little on the stocky side, yet very handsome in an Arab sort of way. In one picture he was visiting an orphanage and a little girl sat smiling on his knee. Another showed the inauguration of a land reclamation scheme and there he was with an Arab headdress wrapped around his head, Iraqi peasant style. In the third, he was at the front playing general, his favorite role. The newspapers were full of his praises and condemnation of the enemy who could be Iran, Israel or the US or any combination of them put together. Was it all real? Did anybody believe it? If they truly believed their attacks on the US, then how could they explain Darrells, me? Brother Barazan, how many governments are there in Iraq?

The lobby of the Mansour Melia Hotel was full of early risers. Most of them were non-Arabs attached to metal briefcases undoubtedly full of irresistible offerings for their hosts. International salesmen always look full of grand expectations. Their sense of self-importance is encouraged, but the whole thing is comical. I was sure there were Yugoslav and Spanish arms salesmen trying to convince them their goods were as effective as those from France and Russia. Probably the same guys went to Iran on different passports. In a remote corner, there were two Lebanese viewing everyone with apprehension and I decided that they had something very Lebanese to hide. What dishonesty were they promoting now?

I moved around the marble lobby without direction, but finally sat down and ordered a cup of Turkish coffee which was served flavored with cardamom seed. The bookstore was closed. I looked at the display windows of the tourist stores and their overpriced imitation native goods, brass and carved wood. There was nothing to do but read and reread the newspapers. This time I noticed that neither the orphanage, the land reclamation scheme or the war front showed clearly; just himself.

At 9:00 a.m., my companion showed up, clicked his heels and sat down next to me. He too had a cup of Turkish coffee and whispered that we would soon be on the move. Ten minutes later we crossed the river towards the presidential palace and began following twists and turns. About three hundred yards from the palace, we ran into a legitimate roadblock manned by men wearing Special Forces uniforms. My companion got out of the car and advised me to do the same and we were both subjected to a body search. Another eighty yards, another roadblock, and this time a metal detector. We reached the last stop and a thorough search was followed by a forty-yard walk to the marble stairs of the palace which was surrounded by barbed wire and other obstacles. Then we went up to the huge door where we earned a salute instead of a search.

My companion stayed with me for about another thirty yards or so, saluted a fully uniformed colonel and introduced me. He then saluted again and turned around military-style without saying a word.

The colonel gave me a brief soldierly welcome, then, erect, led me towards an elevator and instructed the operator to go to the second floor. A twenty yard walk to the right and this time an extremely thorough search of both of us by three men who, once satisfied, knocked at the door and opened it without hearing a command from the inside.

There he was, looking every inch the general he always wanted to be, in full military uniform with his black Special Forces beret strategically placed on top of his desk. He stood straight, unsmiling, his eyes fixed directly on me, examining me from head to toe. It was a huge office, sixty by forty feet. His desk was deep-colored rosewood. There were historical objects on the walls, Arabic scripts and Assyrian warring figurines and a sword, as well as self-serving tributes, pictures of new factories and rural scenes of land reclamation projects. There were portraits of Marouse Affry, founder of the ruling Baath Party, and Ahmed Al Sader, Saddam's predecessor. There was, surprise, surprise, also his own picture. There were expensive-looking, dark leather couches in front of the desk, and coffee tables everywhere covered with brass ashtrays, brass plates and ceremonial coffee pots.

His only concession to my entry was to move to the side of his desk. The colonel led the way, saluted again and mentioned my name. He asked for further orders, but received none. Saddam's voice as he greeted me was clear, without theatricality, the tone of one accustomed to command. He nodded to the colonel who saluted once more, marched backwards towards the door, turned round and made his exit. Saddam gave me a firm hand and I made a symbolic brief bow, then he motioned me to one of the couches. I sat down and he took the one immediately opposite me.

The words could have been delivered by anyone, but the eyes were taking everything in. "I trust your stay here is comfortable. Iraq is your country, the country of every Arab."

"I consider Iraq my country, Mr. President. My stay is most enjoyable and Dr. Najid, and particularly Brother Barazan, have gone out of their way to make it so—as they always do." The rehearsed part came out of sequence, but I retrieved it.

"I am pleased. I will make sure you always have the number of my direct telephone, just in case you need anything. Use it if you want to. I am available to you." This statement required a genuine reaction.

"Mr. President, I am honored. It will be in trust with me and will only be used in situations affecting the national interest." My voice quivered slightly for a moment.

"Was your friend Darrells happy?"

"Yes, sir, very," and I smiled. "I think he demonstrated his happiness through the article he wrote. He is read widely in America. I believe he will do us a lot of good in Washington." And I wondered.

"Tell me about Washington."

"What would the President like to know about Washington?" I wanted to avoid sounding too eager.

Saddam waited for the captain to serve the Turkish coffee. "I want to know why they tell us one thing and then do something else, the opposite. Who runs Washington?"

For a brief moment I tried to look him in the eye to decipher his mood, then I changed my mind. "A lot of people run Washington, Mr. President. It isn't simple. I guess President Reagan does, but he is not totally free. Congress and others have a say about everything. It is the nature of the American system of government."

"Then who do we deal with?" he asked despairingly.

"Unfortunately, we have to live with all of them, but we deal with Reagan's representatives."

A bit of impatience surfaced. "But everyone who contacts us says he is Reagan's representative. Even Darrells told me he could do things for us in Washington. This is why we made our request."

"Mr. President," and I breathed deeply, "it all depends on what

Iraq wants. Different things are done in different ways. In Washington, there is no one person who decides everything. The easiest things to do are those not involving Congress. Forgive me, but half the people in Congress don't know where Iraq is and the other half doesn't want to because of the pressure of the Israeli lobby. What Brother Barazan and Dr. Najid asked for isn't possible. Congress must approve it and Reagan knows they would not, so he won't even ask them for their approval."

"What about helping us against Iran? Khomeini humiliated them with the hostages. We need two things. They must stop the flow of spare parts to Iran and they can let us know whether Russia is providing Iran with satellite pictures of our troop movements. Surely these things can be done without Congress?" Saddam made it clear he had done his homework.

"Those are important requests and you are quite right, sir—Congress wouldn't be involved. I think that Reagan can decide on both by himself. I will tell Darrells. I do believe he is trying to help. He values his connection with you, sir." For a second, I wondered what Darrells would think.

Saddam smiled. "Something else, Daoud, what about going to Washington for us? You seem to get along well with them. You are also a citizen of their country and you know how their government works. We have no ambassador in Washington. We need someone there who will keep us informed of what is happening. You would report directly to my office."

"Mr. President, I'd go anywhere if it helps the Arab cause. My family won't like it, but that is secondary. However, may I suggest we use Darrells to test the water. He will try his best. He wants to be the first US Ambassador to Iraq after diplomatic relations are restored—if they are."

Saddam knew I was improvising; he didn't push. "Okay, try Darrells on these things. Let's find out. And Daoud, don't forget your Arabism. You are one of us, a valued brother. Stay in contact with Barazan on what Darrells has to say. Barazan is in constant touch with me even if I am on the battlefield. No need to inform Dr. Najid and others. Consider this a private visit."

"Yes, Brother President."

"And Daoud, thank you. Thank you for all of us. Iraq will never forget those who stood by it in its hour of need."

Hit back, Daoud, you've rehearsed this part, hit back now.

"Brother President, my service to Iraq is a duty, a source of honor. You have done us proud, sir. The best any one of us can do is to contribute his little bit—miniscule compared to your efforts." I was thinking of what Maggie might say if she heard me being pompous and sycophantic, would she want to know at all?

"Good-bye, Daoud. I will be waiting to hear."

He rose towards his desk and pressed a buzzer. The colonel appeared, saluted and we both backed away to the door, turned around and walked out. No word was said. To the elevator, down the stairs to the outside door where my constant companion was keeping the guards company.

Leaving Saddam's palace is easier than getting into it. The guards didn't do much searching and were happy to wave us through each roadblock. My companion was as silent as the colonel until we had cleared the last check point.

"How was the great leader?" He smiled.

"Magnificent. The Arabs need more like him, but then they don't make them every day. It is him and Nasser in the last thirty years. No one else measures up."

We drove to the Mansour Melia where, much to my surprise, Barazan was waiting for me in the reception area of my suite. He hugged me warmly and patted me on the back, asking, "How did it go?"

"Very well indeed. I am to report to you."

"I know, Daoud, I know. But be careful," and he wagged his long index finger, "there are a few people in Baghdad who spy on who sees the President and they report it to our enemies. They will be after you in London, the pro-Iranians and some misguided Iraqis who follow them. Do you want our boys in London to get you a gun?"

The request woke me up; it always comes down to the gun with this type of government. "No, Brother Barazan. Anyone who wants me dead can easily do the job. I go for walks in Hyde Park. Besides, if you carry a gun you have to be prepared to use it and I'm not ready for that yet."

"You will contact Darrells?"

"Yes."

"Not a word to King Hussein's group. They are infiltrated by the Israelis."

"Not a word. I have no contact with them anyway."

"I meant Darrells shouldn't say anything to them. By the way, you leave at 9:00." He gazed at me.

"Tonight?" I invited him to sit down, but he declined.

He leaned back on his heels. "Yes, there isn't much time to waste."

"I need some nuts and sweets to take home," I said laughing.

"He'll do it." My companion nodded and disappeared right away to get the pistachio nuts for Maggie and some sweets for me. Life is funny when pistachios symbolize one's link with reality, but the elation of my meeting with Saddam was subsiding. My thoughts were turning to making Maggie happy, to home.

Barazan left, and I bathed, took a nap and then went downstairs to the cafeteria for a snack. He had it, Saddam. That special quality that makes for leadership. That power within that makes itself felt in other people, a natural ability to command, to transmit something special which resides in the makeup of great men. Are they born with it, I wondered? How did he arrive at it? Even when he was polite, the aura of his supremacy never left him. I liked him. He listened and understood and legend had it most powerful men didn't. I thought he liked me. He got straight answers, that's for sure. I wondered how all the Lebanese journalists who traveled to his office begging for money to support him behaved when they got there. I thought I had acquitted myself well, perhaps not in a totally Arab way, but well.

The rap on the door was gentle. I opened it to find my companion with two huge sacks, one of mixed nuts, the other of sweets. The nuts always went to Maggie's mother. It was the only link between us. Whenever I took her some nuts, there was always a thank you to the unknown sender.

My companion, undoubtedly following instructions, didn't come with me to the airport, but he did give me the thick envelope, my one way ticket to whoredom.

CHAPTER ELEVEN

Subconsciously Maggie, my own Maggie, was put on the shelf. She could protest all she wanted. What was at stake was much, much bigger. I told myself that Maggie would come round, she would come back to being Maggie, my lover and source of life. But this opportunity was a once in a lifetime. It was time to quench the mental thirst, yes to write history through the back door by serving America and Araby. Maggie was intelligent enough. She would understand how much it meant to me—my one major chance. So the key was to make her see how important it all was, to reach beyond my personal involvement to a bigger picture of religious tyranny. I don't know . . . it will have to wait for now, it will have to wait.

I didn't read for long, or even think. The strain of the meetings began to show and I slept for five of the six-hour Baghdad to London flight. It was seven in the morning when I arrived and I ordered the taxi to Maggie's place at Drove Mews and woke her up with impatient ringing of the door bell. She opened the door and stood there motionless, not a smirk, no movement, practically no reaction. I moved forward and kissed her gently on the lips without getting the slightest response. I moved my suitcase inside and she shut the door behind me. We were at a loss as to what to say to each other.

"Well, here, your mother has a year's supply of nuts." My voice was unnatural.

"Shouldn't have bothered. She eats them all at once and all they do is make her fat." She crossed her arms, stood against the wall of her living room and just looked at me.

"Is it alright if I go upstairs and take a bath?"

"Sure—do what you want." There was still no movement.

"Why aren't you friendly?"

There was cold anger of a type I hadn't seen before. "You didn't tell me you were coming back today. What are you doing? Checking up on me? Are we down to that?"

"Christ, Maggie, what the hell is this?"

"I am sorry, I guess I just don't feel well. Anyway, how is the chief?"

"Unbelievable! He's got it, that bastard. Amazing guy, a real good listener. Not a word too many, not a word too few. Unbelievable." I tried to put a false ring in my voice.

"Did he take care of you the way he buys the people in your favorite whorehouse, the Lebanese journalists? Did he pay you? What next? Arms, spying, both? What are you going to do for El Maximo leader?"

I looked at her blank, unblinking face. "Jesus . . . I've already told you what I am doing. Can I take my bath now?"

"You can go drown for all I care."

"That's not nice."

"It wasn't meant to be." A whisper as she unfolded her arms.

"Okay."

I climbed the stairs to the bathroom I knew so well, undressed and soaked myself back into a state of drowsiness. I got out, ready for sleep and hoped Maggie would join me in bed but she was downstairs dressed and ready to go.

I stopped in the middle of the stairs. "Aren't you coming to bed with me?"

"No, it's my china mending class today. I've got to go now."

"Can't it wait?"

"No."

I shook my head. "Maggie, I missed you, really, really missed you."

"I'll see you later."

"Maggie, please, just when things are coming together for me. Things are really good."

"I just don't know and don't want to know. Don't count on me. China mending makes a hell of a lot more sense. I really thought you were different." She choked back the tears.

"I still love you."

"And I love you, but I can't take it. What is it about? Toy soldiering, your ambition in life to be truly American. You don't want to make history, you want to belong. What we have isn't enough for you." She moved about the room aimlessly, making as if she was kicking her feet up in anger.

Desperate, I wanted to stop things from getting out of hand. "Why don't you stop the words before they come out. You're determined to hurt. Better go to your china mending class. I will be here when you come back. Give us a kiss."

Another slight touching, a tasteless meeting of the lips and she was gone.

I woke up at about three in the afternoon, just in time to telephone Darrells. For someone who hated the instrument so much, this was tantamount to torture, especially from here. I knew how Maggie would feel about using her telephone for this, but I had rushed out of Baghdad to contact him, to speak to him freely, hopefully without someone listening. Maggie's telephone was decidedly safer than mine in terms of bugging and monitoring. One more thing, using her phone was a declaration of independence, a statement against her ability to divert me from my single purpose.

He answered his direct Washington number himself. "Jimmy, it's Daoud. I am back in London."

"Well . . . I bet you're tired. Welcome back to civilization. How was it?"

"Beyond anything I dreamed of. They were full of brotherly Arab love. Himself was very interesting. Christ, I see why you were smitten. He watched me like a hawk. I swear he could hear my heart beat. He likes you very much, but we've got problems." Subconsciously, I was imitating Darrells when he gave a report.

"Like what?"

"Loads—it's heavy stuff, Jimmy, and I'd rather not use the phone. Can you fly over?"

Darrells wasn't about to be summoned. "Not a chance. Try your best and let's see if I can understand you."

"Well, he definitely wants you—us—to be the channel to Washington. He sure doesn't trust King Hussein for a mass of confused reasons. For now, I am to play messenger between you. I don't think they want you there often. In a way they're using me to downplay the contact with the US. Still, we're it. I don't think they're using other channels to Washington, but then you know about that and I don't."

I wasn't about to be allowed to continue. "Daoud, don't get discursive, what is it? What does he want?"

"Basically, two things. No spare parts to Iran. He thinks the US can do more here, perhaps put pressure on the loopholes in Europe. Second, he wants to know whether the Russians are giving Khomeini satellite pictures of the battle front. Christ, if that's true and we can prove it, that's the end of Russia in Iraq. He is already upset over Russia's refusal to give him spare parts for his Migs—much more than he is willing to admit in public."

"He doesn't go for small ones, does he! Does he trust you?" Darrells was reducing things to fundamentals.

"I don't think he gives a damn about me. I think he likes me, but that's not the point. He wants a reliable channel to the US. Gave me a present but, shit, he obviously thinks I work for you and that is really the end of me in terms of commercial or public relations work for them. I feel like a Lebanese."

He cut me short. "Don't be silly, don't let that bother you. I don't think it's that bad, but we will take care of you. Don't worry about that."

"Jimmy, what if a Congressman or another nut says the wrong thing while I'm there. It's my neck you know. The Iraqis are humorless—they change overnight." I became aware that my role was changing without my consent.

"I know, I know. We have to be careful. Can't control some of the idiots on the Hill, but you can count on support from State. I'll take it up with Schmitt directly, I promise. Wasn't he your dean in graduate school?"

"Yes, a damn good dean, actually. He'd remember me. But listen, what about what Saddam wants? They're waiting for an answer."

There was a pause. "Let me check on the picture situation and get back to you. I know the answer about the spare parts, but let's hold back on that and see if we can be more helpful on the satellite pictures."

"Will you call me back? Call me here tomorrow. 631 6645—it's safer than my house. I'm at Maggie's place."

"Does Maggie know any of this?"

"She suspects something is on, but I haven't told her."

"Daoud, careful." I could almost see the look of disapproval on his face.

"She'd never do anything to upset the cart, don't worry. She's trying to get me away from it all—the simple life."

"Still, be careful. All this calling is a bad idea, but we don't want you using normal channels. The moment you feel you are being shadowed, bugged, anything like that, call. Don't call me, call the other number in London and speak to Susie Kerr. Tell her 'my lovers won't leave me alone'. She will pass on the message and we'll take it from there."

"Okay."

Having put me in my place, Darrells resorted to massaging my ego. "What's the matter? You don't sound happy. We'll get something to please your friends and, boy, if we succeed, if we get the Ruskies out of Iraq, then I think you ought to come here for a special thank you from your old dean and the President."

"Yes, Jimmy."

"Don't be surly, damn it. Forget about trading, this is much more important and you've done a great job. We'll always have something for you to do, please accept that."

"I guess it makes sense, but I really want to help them—against Khomeini that is. I think we should."

"There's no problem there. We'll do something for them and you will not be forgotten, I promise. I'll call you tomorrow."

Time to balance the books, to look at what was happening. Saddam and Barazan were convinced I was a US agent. Darrells saw to that. Darrells was using me and why not? He wasn't even paying me a salary. The Iraqis did pay—on an occasional basis. I was in the middle again, riding the fence, feeding my schizoid Arab and American ego. God . . . I wasn't really close to either side. But Maggie . . . what was I going to do about Maggie? A filthy business, a children's crusade, a boy scout parade and Micky Mouse stuff were her names for what was happening. To her it competed with what we had, all this nonsense. She had no craving for money; people born with it seldom do. Glory didn't interest her, nor did glamor. She was losing her man to what she considered a dirty game and that hurt, the game coming ahead of her, the over-whelming urge to meddle obliterating the picture of the man she loved. I never really knew what she wanted me to do, though one time, one time only, she told me I should be near a university, attached to academe, writing about vanishing Bedouin values or something equally esoteric and she had been so reluctant to say it.

On the phone from Baghdad I had thought she would be easy. The hell she was. She was cold, distant and obviously unhappy. Oh, Maggie, just this time. You can't possibly blame me for wanting to be a hero. Everybody wants to be a hero. Why, God damn it, why? I couldn't let her rule me. I couldn't allow her to dictate to me. Bullshit—she wasn't trying to do that. She loves me and simply couldn't relate to it—the business itself and my frustration of being neither here nor there. Why didn't she give in? The Brits never do. Look how they fight and win wars. They dig their heels in and don't give up. The Arab mental agility to accommodate isn't there. I have to be tough with her. Can't keep begging for understanding. Christ—it's rejection. She's miles away. I can't talk to her. She is not going to leave though. Not my Maggie. . . . No, no. . . . Fuck Darrells. Why did he come back? There wasn't a genuine bone in his body, manipulating me. I am already the loser. Saddam and Barazan think my loyalty is to America, the CIA. Jesus Christ Almighty, it isn't. Better think of a good restaurant to take Maggie to. She finds it easier to talk after a few drinks. She never admits it but she does.

Maggie came back. She'd begun her china mending class and had lunch with her sister who took her home to see Theodore, her five year old nephew. They had spent the better part of the afternoon playing with him. I wonder whether she told her sister. She wouldn't. Susanne was ignorant about anything east of Jersey. She'd scream, "Spying—how exciting. Well done, Daoud!" Yup, the whole thing would be "a marvelous good idea".

When she came back, her manner was the same, distant. The kiss of greeting was the same, cold. The news of dinner at Le Souquet made no impression. She fixed herself a cup of coffee and didn't bother offering me one. She was itching for a confrontation. "Did you call Darrells?"

"Yes."

"I knew you would. They'll bug my phone now!"

My voice rose a bit. "Maggie, no one knew I was here and I didn't say much."

"Well, do what you want. I can't stop you."

"Stop me from what? Making money, fighting Khomeini, saving the Arabs, satisfying my ego? None of these things is a crime. I don't have what you have. I don't want to be another middle class slob, I need to do something with my life, to stop floating . . . a bit of meaning." But the drama I tried to muster didn't work.

"What are you doing to us is a crime."

"What am I doing to us, Maggie? I still love you. You love me. I don't know what the hell is bothering you. If I didn't trust you implicitly, I wouldn't have said a word."

"I wish you hadn't."

"So do I, believe me, so do I."

"Your favorite film, *Casablanca*, is on the box. Perhaps you want to watch it while I bathe and change."

"Oh yes . . . play it again, Sam." I mumbled.

Her eyes rested on me. "Yes . . . play it . . . play it again. Remember the ending?"

"Do I? I've seen it over ten times."

"Think about it." She tapped her shoe for emphasis, as usual.

"I do, all the time. But I am the hero of course."

"No, you are not. You want to be the hero, but real heroes are made of different stuff. Ricky wasn't the hero. The other guy, the real guy, Laslou, gets the girl. He is the hero—not the meddler."

"So, so."

"So, to my bath . . . while you see the end of *Casablanca*."

My shout followed her up the stairs. "I'll change the ending."

Good food and wine cannot salvage a condemned evening. All attempts at conversation failed. She wasn't in the mood for theater the following week. Even the scheduled dinner with some old advertising friends had to be cancelled; she wasn't up to it. She was tired and wanted to go to Wiltshire to visit her parents for a week. A bit of fresh country air would lift her spirits, she claimed.

There wasn't a way to reach her. She was in full retreat to a world which she didn't want to share with me. So I accepted her going to Wiltshire, promising to take care of the cats and not drink too much. Sex was completely out of the question and she left the day after, waving a cursory good-bye instead of the usual hug and squeeze.

That afternoon, Darrells, having tried me at Maggie's without success, called me at my place, unable to hide the ring of success in his voice.

"Daoud, Jimmy."

"Yes, how are you?"

"Well, very well. We've hit gold."

"Yeah . . . tell me more."

"The Iranians *are* getting the Russian satellite pictures. We have copies of them. We got them through Iranian Air Force elements. You must get the news to them soonest. The Iranians are massing in the Mesan region, not opposite Basra where our friends are waiting for them, but a hundred miles north. It looks as though they will attack in two days."

Heat rushed to my head. "Jimmy, are you sure? It's my neck. They have to move at least two divisions to Mesan. Jesus wept, if this isn't true, Saddam will get me even if I flee to the moon. Are you absolutely certain?"

"Saw them myself, but we can't release them. They've got to take our word for it."

"What about his other request?"

"Forget about that for now. Get to work. They must know this immediately."

"Okay. I'll call Barazan straight away. This God damned phone business is crazy."

"There's no choice. Don't waste a moment. Bye."

I waited a moment, went through a change of character, picked up the phone and called Baghdad. I no longer cared whether it was bugged.

Barazan was there. "Brother Barazan, it's Daoud. Listen, I must speak to you openly. Is it okay?"

"Just a minute. Go ahead—I'll have it recorded."

"Darrells just called. He has vital news. You must take it to the Brother President immediately."

"What is it?"

My delivery was even, flat, a bit patronizing, an attempt at overwhelming rather than sharing. "The Americans have proof Russia is giving Iran satellite pictures. They have copies of them which they can't release."

"Why not?"

I actually snapped at him. "Never mind that for now—national security or something. The Iranians are massing opposite the Mesan region not Basra. They have about a hundred thousand men there. They could attack as soon as two days. You must do something. This is bigger than the details of why not."

"Is Darrells telling the truth?"

Barazan, you bastard, I thought, you need me now. You need me now. "Yes. They don't want you to lose, damn it. Of course he is telling the truth. You must get this to the President now. I don't have any more news and there isn't time to confirm anything. The Iranians could launch something in Mesan any minute. Darrells says that he saw the pictures himself."

"Stay in your office—is that where you are?"

"Yes."

"Stay there. I will call the President right away."

I waited for Barazan to call back. Every time someone called, I told them to call back later to keep the line free. As we had three telephone lines, it didn't make sense at all, but nobody seemed to notice how jumpy I was. I was doing my job. I knew what I wanted. I wanted to hear about Saddam's reaction. I wanted a message from Saddam saying well done. I was consumed by the importance of the moment and what I had achieved. My God, this was it.

The telephone finally rang and the whisper on the line suggested Baghdad. Barazan's voice came through clearly with a note of undisguised, loud happiness.

"Daoud, your information is true. Our own reconnaissance was beginning to suggest the same thing, a day or two ago. Everything is under control. Daoud, we love you, we love you, we love you. I love you. There is a place for people like you in the history of our glorious nation. The President sends his salutations. He can't wait to see you with us again and please thank Mr. Darrells—he's proved himself. Daoud, do you hear me?"

The Arab in me took over. It was as if I was joining a folk dance. "I hear you and I love you too. I love all of you and I wish I could be with you at the front at this time."

"You are doing enough. I must go. Allah bless you, my brother. Allah bless you and be with you."

"Good-bye, Brother Barazan."

I was tired, spent. Something of my body and soul had been used up and I felt exhausted, empty, depressed. It was as if I wanted the state of tension to continue. I thrived on it. There wasn't much left to do except a call back to Darrells, another use of the telephone to manipulate the world.

"Jimmy, message delivered, accepted with a huge thank you and being acted upon."

"Good lad."

"Good lad, fucking hell." My voice shook with rage.

"What's the matter?"

"I want out. I don't want this. You got me into it. Get me out."

"Listen, you're not back to Beirut again. What are you, a schizoid or something? You are a big boy now."

"I'm a whore, a messenger boy. If I didn't hate Khomeini so much, I wouldn't do it." Aloneness turned into instant blackness and I wanted to cry.

"What's happened to you? You were alright an hour ago."

Where is Maggie? Where the hell was Maggie? "I was free an hour ago. Now I don't know. Barazan told me he loved me."

"I'm sure he does. This ... this is big stuff. You must use it in dealing with them. More money, influence. Get them to give you some contracts. We'll get some British and French companies to appoint you agent so you might capitalize on this."

"I don't want it." I wanted her.

"What the hell do you want then?"

"I want to be in Wiltshire. I want to be in the country looking at flowers."

"You want to be where?" It wasn't a question; it was an order for me to stop it.

"In Wiltshire with my girlfriend."

"Stop being juvenile. I don't even understand you half the time."

"I know you don't. . . ."

"Listen, I've got to go. We all feel funny after a major operation, even when it's successful—post-operative blues."

"Post-operative shit. They love me, wow!"

"I'll talk to you tomorrow about other things."

"I'll be here waiting. Another love message to Barazan."

He tried to make light of it. "Oh, shut up, just shut up. Honestly, go out and get laid or drunk or something, you'll feel better."

"I think I will. I think I'll do both."

Poor Maggie ... poor, poor Maggie. So near and so far away, I thought.

"Good lad."

My scream came out before I could control it. "Jimmy, don't call me lad. I am thirty fucking seven years old and I don't want to be called lad. I feel like a hundred."

"Alright, Daoud. Talk to you tomorrow. You're not making sense now."

I had no meetings scheduled for the following day. This meant I could dispense with the suit and tie and make do with a pair of ivy league type khaki trousers and a sport shirt. I met with Michael, my resident engineer, to advise him about a request from Jordan for electrical switch gear. He was to follow up on it. I also talked to Martin, my other colleague, to see if we could secure the agency of a Finnish paper company for a Kuwaiti trading group. I even dictated unexciting letters to Sue to send to companies who owed us answers on previous projects.

There was the pretense that things were normal and the tantalizing knowledge that Darrells would phone later on in the day. He did, at 3:15 p.m. London time.

"Feel any better?" Reluctantly.

"Not particularly. But I did get a good night's sleep."

"What gets into you? Doesn't success agree with you?"

"I'm being used again and that's what I mind. To hell with Khomeini. I hope someone gets him. But I'm being used by you and I don't like it and then the Iraqis think it's a good idea too. Things were going well with them. I had no need to get into heavy games. The slightest mistake and boom, it's me. Why didn't I just continue to do my small PR work?"

"I told you we will take care of you if need be."

I tried to answer Darrells in the same even voice he was using. "How?"

"We'll always find something for you to do."

"What if I don't want it and I'm left out in the cold?"

"Stop moralizing. It's dog eat dog and you know it. I can't believe half of what you say."

"Okay, okay. What's going on now?"

"His other request—please tell Barazan nothing, but nothing, reaches Iran from us. Not a nut or a screw. The Israelis supply some incidental gear, but can't provide the parts to make Iranian planes airborne without cannibalizing their own and they aren't about to do that. McClane spoke to Begin in very strong terms and he promised to stop helping Iran, but that doesn't mean much. Among his other attributes, Begin is a liar."

"What about the Europeans? A lot of stuff is reaching Iran via Austria and Italy. It's made everywhere, in both Eastern and Western Europe. Can anything be done about that?"

Darrells sighed heavily. "We tried, God we tried. This guy Kreisky in Austria is a pain in the ass, holier than thou and elusive. The Italians need the cash, need oil more probably, and they will barter. We can't control them. We know what they are up to, but how do you get Italians to listen? We've been trying our best."

113

"They don't accept that. They think that you can stop it."

"Well we can't. But there is something we could try. Too delicate for this phone. Where can I call you at 7:00 p.m. your time? Not at Maggie's—somewhere public."

It's about time we became careful. "Try 5893532. It's a pub. Ask for me by name. I'll have pen and paper ready."

Another nerve-wracking wait, another Darrells scheme ... another God damned phone call. What the hell was he up to now? What was so important? I could never predict him. He was inventive, he always had something new up his old sleeve.

I was at the pub at 6:00 p.m. and the lousy telephone kept ringing, but not for me. Seven meant seven to Darrells—not five to seven or five past seven. And so it was, a ring at seven and a shout from behind the bar that it was for me and I rushed into the booth, turned the light on and waited for the click of the receiver at the other extension.

"Okay Jimmy, what is it?"

"Listen carefully."

"I always do, one of my problems."

"We know about the major shipments to Iran. Our boys in Europe keep a close watch on Iranian operations and purchases."

"Yes. . . ."

"What if we told the Iraqis about them, would that work?"

"So what! They know all about that. They're the ones who told me about Austria and Italy."

"No, no, we tell them about Iranian arms purchases in detail, then they go to work and blow them up, or divert them on the high seas, or stop them when crossing the Suez Canal. If they have all the details, they could do something to disrupt the flow of hardware to the other side." Silence prevailed.

"Hell, Jimmy, one job like that and not a single Iraqi would be allowed to travel to Europe. They need to get around to buy their own stuff. Besides, they are going through an image change—want to be good guys."

"It doesn't have to be obvious. Perhaps the Iraqis can do it with little or no violence in a way that won't reflect on them. I'll give you an example. Take it down. TMIA, the Italian arms maker, just struck a deal with the Iranians for 150,000 155mm shells at $325 apiece. The goods are about ready in Northern Italy and preparations are being made to ship them to Iran. These goods were purchased against Nigerian papers, End User Certificates, all arranged by a British company which bribed Nigeria's Chief of Staff and Defense Minister. The ship is ostensibly going to Nigeria, but will divert to the Black Sea, and then by truck to Iran."

"This is huge stuff. Can we do anything ourselves?" We both allowed the slip of tongue to pass.

"We can stop it—if the Iraqis cooperate. We have contact with TMIA. Some of their officials will help us, but there is no way we can pay them. They want millions. The Iraqis must pay."

"How do we start?"

"Speak to Barazan and talk him into cooperating with us. They've got to move their asses. A man by the name of Harry Butcher will visit you at your office tomorrow."

"What time?"

"Afternoon."

"Okay I'll make it free, but one more thing, why didn't you call me at home with this one?"

"Never mind that. I'll explain when I see you. Don't worry."

How do you go back from that type of conversation to others starting with, "Do you remember when Whiskey Charlie got so drunk he fell off the bar stool"? But I did. Stayed in the pub two more hours drinking yet more vodka and soda and went home to feed the cats and clean up after them. A call to Maggie was out of order; it was late and would disturb her elderly parents. Barazan had to wait till the morning. Impatiently, I went to bed.

In the morning, I cut short my usual routine and went to the Trafalgar Square post office to place a call to Barazan. I recited my handwritten notes of the telephone conversation with Darrells.

Barazan thanked me for being careful, but wanted time to discuss the offer with "The Brother President". He couldn't commit himself but went as far as admitting the shipment must not reach Iran. He was a little uneasy about resorting to violence and he indicated as much when he was thinking out loud and asked me what I thought.

I told Barazan that our number one job was to verify the existence of the goods and to do that I needed to go to Milan as soon as possible with a helper to check on all the details. Perhaps there was a way to do it without violence. Barazan said that he was in favor of the trip to Milan, but would give me final instructions later.

To act busy, to pretend other things mattered was a problem. The adrenaline was flowing. The urge to call Maggie was resisted. We didn't lie to each other and I didn't want to upset her by telling her how things were, in case she asked. If she were to call, it would be different, it would open the door for social chatter, but if I did I'd have to go right into it. So no call to Maggie. Nothing. Just attempts at reading and then tidying my desk, waiting for Barazan to ring. Two hours of suspended animation, then the phone.

"Daoud, listen carefully. The President is sceptical. Why are the Americans so forthcoming all of a sudden? Just as I expected, you are to verify the existence of the goods and work out a plan for either a take out or diversion to Egypt. We can't use the 155 ourselves. But no violence. Go down to the Latin country. Gazzaz will give you money and anything else you need." Saddam's suspicious mind was beginning to make an appearance.

"I don't need it. I'll use my own and then we'll go. I will have an American with me. He isn't a troublemaker. We'll find some way."

"Be very careful. The Latins have been very good to us. We don't want them upset."

"Trust me."

"We do. Allah be with you."

"Allah protect you, good-bye."

I took Michael and Martin to a local wine bar for a light lunch. We indulged in shop talk. We had to find a good company to work with a Saudi associate to maintain schools and hospitals. The building and equipping programmes were over, but the Saudis were having problems in the maintenance area. Because of the language difficulties, Far Eastern companies couldn't compete and the Americans were too expensive. The Brits were naturals. Martin was going to start his search for such a company, a cleaning and electro-mechanical maintenance company. The jokes about how unclean and unmaintained Britain was came naturally and livened the conversation.

When I returned to the office, I told Sue I was expecting a visitor, but would answer the door myself when the bell rang. She looked puzzled, but agreed.

I watched Harry Butcher climb the steep stairs two at a time. He wanted to make it obvious that he was in very good physical shape. I ushered him into my office and closed the door. I had a good look at him as I motioned to him to sit down. He was American alright, blue blazer, buttoned-down Oxford blue shirt, and gray trousers an inch and a half above his brown shoes. At least six foot two, he had brown hair cropped short, military-style, and narrow shifty eyes. I guess he was handsome in a clean-cut American way. He spoke first.

"Is your office clean?"

"Far as I know."

"Who is in the other offices?"

"My colleagues. They know nothing about this. Sit down please."

"Darrells sent me."

"I know. Would you like a coffee?" I turned to him after we got our coffee. "Tell me about TMIA."

"I thought he told you."

"On the phone . . . very little."

"That's it, that's all I know." He was going to be difficult.

"Are you in touch with the TMIA people?"

"Yes, with the top man. Not top man with TMIA, the top man with the group trying to help us. He is the third man in TMIA."

"Do you trust him?"

"Yes."

"Why?"

"Money—you ought to see him. He wants to make money, you can tell."

"Can I see him?"

"I don't think it's necessary, but yes. My instructions are to do what you want." His nervous eyes continued to examine my office, particularly the curtains.

I told Butcher that we should go to Milan the following day and that our preliminary purpose was to verify the existence of the goods. I also told him that no violent means were to be used. He made some cynical all-American comment about the Iraqis' opposition to violence, refused to telephone his contact from my office and declined money for the tickets saying he would arrange them and the hotel reservations his own way without my help. Butcher's job, as he saw it, was to prove to me and the Iraqis that the deal was for real. He wasn't ready to do anything else without instructions from his "bosses". He capped the whole thing by describing the Iranians and Iraqis as "gooks".

We parted on the promise that Butcher would confirm every-thing soon. After half an hour, he did and we agreed to leave the following morning, stay in Milan for one night, preferably away from busy places.

We agreed to meet at Heathrow at 9:15 a.m. for a 10:00 a.m. flight to Milan. The Al Italia desk. Everything was set.

But Milan was three months ago, a lifetime really and the stewardess just reminded me to buckle my seatbelt for landing in Washington. Yes, I am in Washington to see Brandt to discuss Dr. Raji's visit. Milan was Darrells' show, but this new play is directed by Brandt who will decide where I fit in. . . . Yes, better forget about Milan and the past and start thinking about Brandt and the big game Washington is playing.

CHAPTER TWELVE

The formalities at Dulles International Airport didn't take long. Looking through the windows of the taxi was like a dream because I had difficulty in believing that I was there, yet the buildings and monuments along Washington's wide streets provoked thoughts about America and American history, a longing closer to a naturalized citizen than to those who take their Americanism for granted. All my heroes made appearances: Jefferson, Lincoln, Kennedy and Martin Luther King and I couldn't help but feel a twinge of pain at the thought that my activities wouldn't appeal to any of them, with the possible exception of Kennedy. Yes, there was a delicious unreality about Washington, perhaps about all of the American experience and this trip was a small unreality inside the big one.

It was four in the afternoon when the taxi dropped me in front of The Four Seasons Hotel. Funnily, I could hear Arabic being shouted with a Palestinian accent in the gas station across the street which made me linger a minute before entering the place and registering. I tipped the porter who took me to my room, waited for him to exit and dialed Brandt.

"Bill, I just got in. It will take me ten minutes to shave and freshen up, then I'm yours."

He was especially bland. "Welcome to Washington. Take your time. Take a taxi when you're ready and come right over. It's best if we meet here."

"Okay, I'll be with you in about half an hour."

"Take your time."

The trip to Brandt's office took only five minutes more than promised. There was a fleeting thought about the characterless modern four-story building with no signs and how it related to the CIA. I was ushered into the small office to face a jacketless Bill Brandt in a short-sleeve shirt. We shook hands warmly but correctly, after which he ordered us two coffees, wasted the time waiting for them with conversation about the boring flight, then closed the door.

Alone at last, he gave me a truly friendly smile. "Well my boy, excitement seems to follow you everywhere. This is quite a thing, Raji himself calling on you. We had lost track of him, but how clever of them. Tell me everything in the minutest details, even his gestures, and if you don't mind I'll just make notes as you go along—I don't like taping things. We've got plenty of time unless you have something to do."

I recreated the Raji visit, emphasizing his elegance, the over-whelming impressions and sense of urgency he imparted, the speed with which he plunged into things and the deliberateness of it all. At the end I saw fit to editorialize, telling Brandt that while my duty compelled me to do what I did, I was dead set against any involvement beyond transmitting the Raji message. Brandt set down his pen and looked at me as if to say he understood and sympathized, then the old pro in him took over. "Few questions, Daoud, if you don't mind. Do you know where your brother is and what he's up to? You may not wish to answer."

I shrugged my shoulders and allowed my lower lip to stick out. "Bill, I don't. I haven't seen him or heard from him in two years. Ask Cape Miller—he was trying to bribe them to stop highjacking and blowing up planes."

"Let's not go off on a tangent. What about this business of going to Jerusalem—how do you feel about that?"

"Like any Palestinian, I'm not immune. I was a bit awed by the simplicity of purpose. . . ." I didn't need to say more.

"Do you believe the reasons for Raji's visit—what he told you?"

I moved my head a little backward and pretended to think. "Yes, they are hurting, Bill. They need to re-engine all their British Chieftain tanks, no substitute engine will do, and Thatcher refuses to sell. Also all the cylinders, the gun barrels on the M60 tanks they bought from us are worn out. In other words eighty percent of their tank force is immobilized, useless. They need ammo for their 130, 155 and 175mm guns. They're in trouble, no doubt about it. But then is Raji's visit about that? I don't know. Perhaps someone convinced him I am the right channel to reach Washington . . . I mean this place. I just don't know. We need Darrells' devious mind."

Brandt was deep in thought. "Either that or your little brother can shed some light on things."

Involuntarily I interrupted. "Wait a minute, Bill. There is more to it than that. We're dealing with two distinct things. The first has to do with me, why they came to me, but the second part is beyond that. Obviously Raji expects a friendly response from here, from you. What gave him the idea that you'd be receptive? Who? Don't tell me, but this little fellah has the feeling that you guys have been doing a good job playing both sides against the middle. Either Tehran didn't like the old channel it was using or something happened to it, that's why Raji came to me, but your—the contact with them isn't new—right? I mean he pretty much said that."

A patronizing smile surfaced. "You know, in spite of the Saddam disaster and the coolness between you, Darrells thinks you're the best field analyst we ever had. I think he's right. It's almost like a second nature to you. I wish the Beast had some of that."

"Who's the Beast?"

"Never mind. How are you, in yourself, Daoud?" The well-brought up boy took his time before becoming personal.

"I'm well, but let's talk about the Beast for a minute. Did the Beast tell you about Zayed and the chemical plant? Is that why things came to an end through that channel? Please don't answer me, but you should know that they think Zayed is an Iraqi and that he is in jail. They have no idea that he's a Palestinian and is in London."

Brandt's lazy voice meted the words out one at a time. "Where is Zayed in London?"

"He lives around Holland Park, spends his time with Banal Nagil, the former Palestinian spokesman at the UN, the guy Darrells and I got back in Beirut. Is that what happened Bill, did we use Banal to get Kalam Zayed? This is more twisted than I thought."

Brandt made that promissory look of sympathy again and I wished he'd answer me, but he didn't. Instead, he clasped his hands behind his neck, leaned back and asked if I'd mind transmitting a simple message to Raji to meet him in London. I agreed and we spoke about how and when and expenses, but said nothing about what would happen afterwards, where I would fit in. A very tired, preoccupied Brandt apologized for not dining with me, but suggested I stay in Washington a day or two to relax and see the sights.

I had nowhere to go in Washington so I had dinner in my room, abusing the television set constantly to take in as much of the thirty-some programming alternatives as possible. Even the television commercials appeared to be reeducating me in things American, adding to the thirst which came to life during my taxi journey and reinforcing the dream like quality of my presence in Washington.

I was leaving the following day and the concierge managed to get me a seat on the overnight special. This gave me a chance to do something about the incipient conversation Brandt kept promising, to challenge his implicit decision to exclude me in this way. I decided to leave traces behind telling how I really was. I did it through raiding the minibar of all the vodka it had, ordering more from the bar, then having a bottle of wine on top. Someone would notice the debris of drinking and Brandt would know the moment they got the bill. Someone would think they had made a great discovery and send a pompous cover note about my suspect state of mind.

As often in London, I lay on the bed and viewed the white ceiling as a screen against which I projected my thoughts three and four hours at a time. The more immobile I am, the clearer my mind projects. I had been doing this on a daily basis, mostly upon returning from the pub at night, but why not here, why not in Washington DC? Will this screen produce a better image, will the pieces of the jigsaw come together?

Where was I now? Yes, back to three months ago and the most unattractive Mr. Butcher, the hoodlum who lived on the periphery of the intelligence world, the tough guy of the Darrells–Daoud Milan operation to save Iraq and make Iran look foolish. The Butchers of this world never confine themselves to their briefs; characteristically they always try to apply simple, violent, superficially attractive solutions to problems they don't understand, and God knows they understand very little.

Yes, time to go to Milan after telling Sue, Martin and Michael I was going to Wiltshire to see Maggie and didn't wish to be disturbed there. They didn't believe me. They felt something odd was afoot, but Iraq was my baby and I often kept things from them, except for financial matters. Meanwhile they ran the everyday business without asking questions.

That evening before the Milan flight, I prepared my overnight bag and then went to the pub. I didn't call Maggie. I didn't want to enter into any discussions or arguments. I was happy talking about when Whiskey Charlie fell off the stool and I bought myself enough vodka and soda to ensure sleep and returned home to my feline companions, Ecstasy and Blacks. Sue was to take care of them while I was gone as she had done in the past.

Butcher was at the Al Italia counter. He had two club class tickets and we checked through customs and immigration without saying a word to each other, though I wished to God that he would stop giving the world his furtive, I've-got-a-secret look. They called the plane and we headed to the boarding gate, still without saying a word. There wasn't much point in speaking in the rush, push and shove of seat allocation.

Breakfast interrupted our newspaper reading. Butcher used the opening to speak—with a military scowl. "My contact at TMIA is not happy you're coming to Milan. He doesn't want too many people involved." It sounded like a reprimand, a bad start.

"Your contact, whoever he is, can stuff it. We are the only customer in town and we've got to determine the whole thing is for real. It can't be done any other way, Harry." The terse answer failed to end the conversation.

"He trusts me—why don't you?"

"That's not the point. I'm responsible to the other side. If anything goes wrong, then it's my stupid Arab head. It can't be done any other way. Either your contact convinces us that the goods exist beyond a shadow of a doubt, or no deal. Where are we staying and when do we meet your man?"

"We are at the Palace. He'll be in touch. We'll meet in the afternoon."

"Okay."

We went back to our newspapers. We didn't like each other. He thought I was haughty. I thought he was a thug, probably an ex-marine selected for tough jobs, a minor field man, a leg man trying to push his way into higher things. I wondered how he felt about taking orders from an Arab, a gook, but didn't ask him. Screw him. The hostility lasted through lunch and the rest of the flight. It was a relief to retreat to my hotel room to lose myself in *Moby Dick*. It was better that way, to keep my distance and merely tell Butcher I'd be waiting for his call.

When finally the telephone rang, I dressed as fast as I could and rushed down to room 312. Butcher was still in his blazer and in the corner, on what looked like a straight comfortable chair, sat Dr. Pietro Napolini who introduced himself with a proper shake of the hand, a polite nod and sat down.

The Doctor was five feet tall, maybe five foot one. He was impeccably dressed—a greenish tweed sports jacket, brown trousers and a beautifully knotted tie. The shirt was unmistakably silk. His shoes shone care and quality.

"Whose room is this?" I asked.

"I booked it," answered Dr. Napolini.

"Sorry, Doctor, we must go somewhere else." I refused to sit down.

He looked at Butcher in bewilderment. "Don't you trust me?"

Butcher shuffled his feet, but I plowed right ahead. "Let's not waste time, Dr. Napolini. I'm not willing to discuss anything here," I answered.

"Where then?"

"In the café down the street. I took a stroll after Harry and I arrived."

"But it's full of people."

Thinking of Darrells' maxim about open places being the best for secret meetings, I decided to tease the Doctor. "Are you being followed?"

"No."

"Then why worry? A café full of people is the best place."

Manicured hands clasped in front of him, the Doctor spoke with the steady voice of someone who had done this before. "I don't like to be treated like a criminal."

His perfunctory complaint got a similar answer. "You are not, sir, but Harry here knows how important this is. We must be careful. One can never be careful enough."

"Okay."

Uneasy with each other, we left the room and followed the odor of fresh roasted coffee. At a corner table Butcher and I ordered beer, the Doctor sherry. Everyone was in character.

I opened: "Doctor, has Harry told you who I am?"

"No."

I clasped my hands in front of me on the table and spoke right at him. "I am from the Iraqi side, but I am also an American and won't do anything except with Uncle Sam's approval. Harry, perhaps you can do the preamble. Tell the Doctor our position."

Butcher complemented my statement with a military-type brief. "Well Dr. Napolini, Daoud's friends are interested in stopping the goods from reaching Iran, but it must be done without any violence. The Iraqis don't want the goods, can't use them. Either they are sunk or we send them to Egypt. The Egyptians can use 155s. Also, the price. There is a difference of opinion on the price."

I wanted to stop Butcher from grovelling to the nattily dressed Doctor. Americans don't know how to behave in the presence of establishment Europeans; they become self-conscious.

"Let's backtrack, Harry. How do you know the goods are there?" I said and turned to Butcher deferentially.

The Doctor reached into his inside pocket and produced his Italian passport and copies of five telexes. He opened the passport to a particular page and handed it over to me. On that page was stamped an Iranian visa numbered 7355 and issued in Rome on 23.4.83. It was valid for one month, but was renewable.

The telexes varied. Four of them came from Colonel Yazdani, Chief of Procurement, Iranian Forces. The fifth was from Colonel Azizi signed on behalf of Yazdani. They all dealt with the order for 150,000 155mm shells. A letter of credit had been opened and extended and had now expired. The last telex promised to reextend the letter of credit. The answerback on all telexes was Iran MOD. I thought the Doctor was telling the truth, but I asked Butcher if Yazdani or Azizi had been verified by Washington. He said they had. I gave the papers back to the Doctor and thanked him for his confidence.

"Well, Doctor, you are not doing this for your health. What is the damage?"

"What do you mean, sir?" This time there was a touch of genuine apprehension.

"I mean, how much money do you want?" He made me smile, the Doctor.

"We told Mr. Butcher. We need thirty percent of the market value of the goods. About fifteen million dollars."

"Doctor, that's a lot of money," I said, putting my glass down.

"It's a big job. It could change the course of the war." This was accompanied with a very Italian hand gesture, the first of the day.

"Nowadays every deal is supposed to change the course of the war. Anyway, what do you say to the fact that we don't want anyone killed or maimed?"

"We can do that. First you will pay up front."

Butcher pounced on the opening. He had been waiting. He announced that he was in charge of what happened to the goods and that he had spoken to "our mutual friend" that afternoon. Openly, crudely, he told me that my job was to take care of the money, to agree on the amount and arrange payment and that all else was up to him.

I snapped, "Harry, these things are one and the same. You can't separate them. Before I go back to ask for the money, I must be able to tell them how it's going to be done."

Butcher and I were arguing in front of the Doctor. He didn't mind, but I did. Butcher had pulled a dirty trick on me. I had to do something, so I spoke to the Doctor.

"Doctor, we will not pay a penny in advance. If the job is done, then we will pay. I am far from agreeing to the fifteen million, but whatever figure they—my group—agree to, the job first, then the payment."

"Signor Daoud, let's finalize the system first. How and when will you pay? If you do not pay anything in advance, then we need a guarantee. That guarantee can be anything. It can be you. Your friends can transfer the money into an escrow account in a bank in Lugano in your name. You provide us with proof that the money is there, then we will keep you with us until the job is finished and you can release the money to us. If we do the job and the money is taken away, is no longer there for you to pay, then it's your life. If it goes through, then all is well and we release you. We will provide full evidence that the job was completed."

"What evidence, Doctor? I'm sorry, but it has to be conclusive. My friends have reason to be suspicious—they've been cheated before." I thought about the number of times both sides in the Gulf War had been cheated.

The soft, gentle, aristocratic voice continued with the utmost politeness. "We will sink the ship. Perhaps we will produce the captain or another person or the stories in newspapers would be enough. If we hand it over to the Egyptians, then your friends must arrange the publicity. Don't they want that?"

"Let me try to move things forward. I don't mind being held a hostage and the proof sequence and though it's obvious I could be coerced into things while being held by you, I accept. But the amount of money is too much. I must go back to them. How much time do we have?"

"A week at most."

"Doctor, you will hear from Butcher within a week."

The Doctor left by himself. Butcher and I walked back to the hotel again without saying a word to each other. We had crossed swords in public and it confirmed our dislike for each other. He told me he'd be busy that evening seeing an old friend and I was relieved. I didn't like the illiterate bastard, though I had the strange feeling my offer to be taken hostage made him see me in a different light, it appealed to his manic makeup and it had almost silenced the Doctor.

I placed a call from the hotel to Darrells in Washington. Almost angrily I asked him to come to London the following day. I complained about Butcher and how difficult he was and insisted that a face-to-face meeting was in order. I concluded that I was, in all likelihood, on my way to Baghdad in two or three days. I underplayed the hostage-taking part by saying it would be circumvented.

Darrells ignored my complaint, but wanted to know if I was confident of securing a positive response from the Iraqis. I said I could, but that I did mind Butcher undermining me publicly and that both Butcher and Darrells should remember that I wouldn't be pushed around. After all, my loyalty was to the Iraqis, just in case he insisted on forgetting.

Darrells said he'd be in London late the following morning, then he acidly inquired as to whether "Wiltshire" would be back or whether I would be alone.

That did it. I couldn't help it. "I will be alone, thank you. And, by the way, that comment was uncalled for. Wiltshire is none of your fucking business."

This time he hit back. "I accept that, though I mind your unnecessarily crude language. Don't make it my business."

"See you tomorrow. We'll be back in London at noon."

A restless, uneasy night at the Milan Palace, in spite of an earlier decision to forget Maggie for now. First Darrells, and then to Baghdad. Maggie, Maggie, Maggie—don't, just don't do it. Come back and hold my hand and let some comfort slip through your fingers. Come back and say anything. Come back, God damn it, and make love to me like old times. Save me from this mad ego trip. They are about to claim me. I have you and only you. Talk to me about growing up in South America, about the rose garden, about mending china. Tell me you're with me. Support me, damn it. I don't even remember what it was like before you. Maggie, my mother, father, sister, brother, lover, please, please come back. Jesus Christ, how dare he talk about Wiltshire. That's you, that's holy, that is mine, mine, mine. Maggie, please my love, don't go away. Come back Maggie, you're mine, don't go away. If only you had met the Doctor. Underneath all that neatness, a killer, a born killer. He wants me as a hostage and I am going to do it. To hell with switchgear for Jordan, I am going to do this, I am, I am. I have to finish this job. This is the last one. Basically, you're right, but it has gone too far to be stopped—not that I really want to stop it. Oh Christ Maggie, won't you just understand!

Butcher and I met in the lobby of the hotel at eight and took a taxi to the airport. We still didn't have much to say to each other and what little there was didn't make polite conversation.

"Will you get me an answer within a week?" he inquired.

"I will give it to Darrells."

"Why Darrells?"

"He's coming to see me. I asked him to. He came to London on the first plane last night. Should have left about 7:00 p.m. Washington time."

"Why didn't you tell me?"

I pretended to read the newspaper. "Because it is none of your business. Our assignment is over the moment we put into London. Darrells and I will deal with it after that. I don't know who issues orders to you and I don't care, but I will not be undermined in public. There is a price for that."

"I see our Arab is hurt—pride and all," he snickered.

"Butcher, I am as American as you are except I can't become President—naturalized citizens can't. The way things are, I don't think there is any difference between us and you can do me a big favor and disappear after we hit London."

"Funny, I feel the same way."

"Good. I'll start now. I'm going to a seat in the back to read."

I got up and left him alone.

"It's been nice."

"My ass it has. Bye Butcher."

"Bye. Remind me not to keep your uncharming company in the future."

"Ta ta."

You wouldn't think grownups up to their ears in derring-do behaved like this. Believe me they do. Not only did the CIA boys in Beirut come near to wearing badges for cover half of the time, but Darrells frequented small, dingy bars near the St. George Hotel to pick up young boys. And a fellow by the name of George Minkney Rayat had a habit of leaving his notes behind with C.N. in front of every name and a telephone number. C.N. stood for code name. Yes Maggie, it is Mickey Mouse stuff.

I was in South Audley Street before I knew it. I was imagining how Wiltshire was and singing its praises, thinking of how nice it would be to settle there and leave this stupid business behind.

Darrells telephoned soon after my arrival. It was another summons to the Dorchester Hotel. He looked a little tired. At his age, overnight transatlantic flights take their toll; the small wrinkles become deep folds like trouser pleats. This didn't phase Darrells though, and he wanted to plunge right into discussing the Milan trip. Tiredness made him stiff and unfriendly. The friendliness of the past two meetings had disappeared. He shook hands politely and ordered coffee for both of us.

"What are you going to do?" he demanded.

"Do about what?" I continued to pretend that I was angry.

"The Doctor, Butcher, the whole operation. We'll release you from this hostage idiocy, but we can't do more than that. It's up to them. If you convince them and they play, then you're dealing a body blow to the whole Iranian war effort. It's all up to your side. What more does Saddam want?"

I wasn't in any mood for the usual Darrells game. "I'm not worried about Baghdad. I think I can manage it. I've already told my secretary to contact the Iraqi Cultural Center and get a ticket for Baghdad tomorrow. I must know what Butcher is going to do. He is a hoodlum, that guy. We don't want anyone killed or injured."

"It's agreed Daoud. They will just sink the ship and everyone escapes—if none of the crew resists. Leave that to me."

Suddenly I was shaking. "Jimmy, it's not on. How are you going to organize that? A whole ship is blown to bits and everyone is safe? It wouldn't look real. Then if we involve so many people someone will talk and the whole thing will lead to me. I like my Goddamn life. I don't want to spend the rest of it looking over my shoulder. You must find a better way, preferably without Butcher. The guy is a one-way ticket to a scandal, perhaps a congressional investigation. And he'd love that—would tell the world what he did to serve flag and country."

"I'm not having you dictate to us on personnel. Butcher is our responsibility. We will deliver the goods to Egypt instead, divert the ship, or, better still, have the Egyptians intercept it. The Egyptians will play, but what about the money?"

"I'll talk to Barazan tomorrow. I should go back and telephone him. He doesn't know I'm coming."

"Listen, Daoud. You've got to talk Barazan into doing this one regardless of cost. I've convinced Washington to help them and this is only the first one, a test case. We are gathering information on all of Iran's current arms deals in Europe. We believe we can stop most of them if Barazan cooperates."

I had to persist. "How? They're short of cash. They can't keep paying this type of money for stuff they can't use. They have to buy for their own use as well."

"Well, I've thought about that, too. The best and cheapest way is to use the press, publicity. The moment we learn about a deal, we leak the story to the press with all the details. That should have a disruptive effect. We've got many news organizations who would play."

"Why not do this now?"

"No. In this case we must pay them for the 155mms altogether. We gave our word to the Doctor and his boys that they would make some money. You don't know how badly Iran needs them. They're beginning to run short. They're paying well over the going price. Back to where we were. There are also the banks. Most of the payment for these goods is made through letters of credit to Swiss banks. The goods are described as something else. If we can show the Swiss banks the letters of credit are for arms, they'll pull out. This is particularly true if we can suggest that helping Iran in this way would jeopardize their relationship with other Arab states. Saudi Arabia and Kuwait, etc."

The enormity of it made me reel. "This is a whole program."

"You bet it is. You are a big man now. You've got to convince them that the Agency and State Department want to help them, that we're really worried about Khomeini because you can kiss the whole damn Middle East good-bye if Iraq falls. Do you think they'll see the light or are we going to get another Saddam tirade about our double-dealing?"

"I'll try, but you better find me a job after this. Let's face it, I can't go back to the old stuff." I was making an indirect apology.

"Don't worry, we won't let you down. And don't use the phone on this one. Wait until you see him in person."

"Don't promise, Jimmy. How long have we known each other? There have been promises to a lot of people all the way back to Zahle. It doesn't make me breathe easier."

That stunned him—momentarily. He was angry, but he stopped short of responding. We shook hands and I walked to South Audley Street.

I hadn't heard from Maggie. She hadn't telephoned. I didn't even try to reach her. I couldn't cope with the two or three opening sentences I would have had to exchange with her mother or father. They always behaved as if something weird was happening whenever I called. Never mind, I'll settle things with Maggie later—whenever that might be.

I tried to call Barazan to tell him I was coming, but couldn't get through to Baghdad. I was going anyway. Must subscribe to the Doctor's rigid time scale. I didn't think it would be possible, but if the delay was a matter of a day or two then the Doctor would have to accept it.

Another pub evening and the bother of packing and to London's Heathrow Airport two hours before the departure of the British Airways flight to Baghdad. No Iraqi Airways VIP treatment this time, but the plane took off right on schedule at 12:30 a.m.

There were only two other people in the first class cabin. They were Iraqis, an elegantly dressed couple. I wondered if they were from the landed gentry of the *ancien régime* or whether they were related to one of today's Iraqi leaders. We didn't speak to each other.

Saddam's International Airport was the same. No one was

waiting for me and it took ages to clear my luggage and get a taxi to the Mansour Melia Hotel. The desk clerk said the place was full, but a word with the manager placed me in the same suite I had occupied the time before, though I could tell he was wondering why I was unaccompanied. The only time a Third World country operates in an organized way is for the people in power or their friends.

I telephoned Barazan's office the first thing the following morning and spoke to an officer there who recognized my name. Barazan was at the battle front, that's all he could say. An excuse to reach himself. I got my diary and dialed the President's private number. My old friend the colonel answered. Unfortunately, the President too was away, though there was no specific mention as to his whereabouts. I assumed he was at the front as well.

This wasn't a subject to discuss with Dr. Najid, my remaining high level contact. After all, the President had been explicit about not wanting him involved. In the end there wasn't anything else to do but wait, I couldn't even go back to the colonel in the President's office.

I telephoned the offices of the President and Barazan the following day and received the same answers. The time to tell Darrells had come. The Doctor had given me one week to obtain approval and organize the money. If things were moving we could ask for extra time, but all I was doing was reading whatever paperbacks I could find on the hotel's newsstand.

Telephoning Darrells without Barazan knowing about it would be dangerous. Some lowly official at the PTT might decide it was a suspicious conversation, repeat it to the secret police and cause an incident before I could reach someone who would understand. A stupid but dangerous situation was developing. Without the presence of the two most important men in the country I was inoperative and indeed highly vulnerable.

As agreed with Darrells, I was to try to use the telex to relay messages, but there was no specific code. I finally composed a telex and convinced myself Darrells would decipher it. It read:

22335 ONWARD (LONDON)
ATTENTION: SUE
PLEASE SEND MAGGIE A DOZEN ROSES TO LINTON,
WILTSHIRE, WITH THE FOLLOWING MESSAGE: YOU ARE

MY DADDY AND MY MUMMY AND WITHOUT YOU ALL IS
WORTH NOTHING. ALL IS WELL IN BAGHDAD BUT MY
DADDY AND MUMMY ARE NOT WITH ME AND I AM
LONELY.
LOVE DAOUD.

The operator rang me at half past two in the morning with an
apology, announcing that there was a call for me from London. It
was Darrells.

"Listen, your secretary got the roses to Maggie. As long as daddy
and mummy are out, why don't you come back tomorrow? I mean
later on today. Leave your things behind. I will meet you at the
airport and then you can turn around and return. It is important."

"That important?" I said, trying to suppress a natural yawn.

"Yes, God damn important. Do it. I will call Sue first thing in the
morning and she will arrange a ticket for you and tell Gazzaz to
organize a visa. It's a must."

"If it is, then I'll do it. If you don't hear from me, then I'm on Iraqi
Airways."

"See you tomorrow."

"Yes."

I couldn't go back to sleep. Had Butcher blown it? Was it already
too late for the Doctor? What could possibly move Darrells to
such action? It was out of character. But then he wanted me back.
That son of a bitch, there was just no end to his scheming. I
wondered what had happened. I wonder if he sent the flowers to
Maggie? He'd gone into the office alone at night, per agreement,
using the spare key I had given him and read the telex. Sue knew
nothing about this, so the message was sent to Maggie. Was she
upset? Was she worried? I thought she'd be upset. All the way
to Baghdad without the courtesy of a telephone call, another
small violation of the way we treated each other. And now this
compulsion to draw her in. There must have been a different way
to signal Darrells without involving her, but inexplicably I wanted
her involved.

When the bookshop opened in the morning I went downstairs
for a new paperback. I bought an old one called *Candle for a Dark
Journey* by a fellow named Carter Brown. The title appealed. It
didn't do much beyond that, a second-rate detective novel, but
then I needed a diversion to waste the time. I told the manager of

133

the hotel to keep my suite for me, but that I would be away for a day. I said nothing about going back to London.

The hours passed slowly and I began to wonder about the wisdom of going to Saddam International Airport without luggage. What would the security people think? Would they be suspicious? Anything unusual aroused their suspicion, fed into their ignorant fears. Besides there certainly is something odd about going to London without luggage.

It was seven in the morning and I had been up for seventeen hours and was very tired. Time to go to the airport. I hated the place, all the disorganized hustle and bustle and noise. I hated all airports, but Saddam International and Heathrow deserved contempt and they were the ones where I seemed to have been living lately.

We got aboard the plane at 11:00 p.m. and I swallowed five aspirins I had bought at the hotel odds and ends store. I knew this time sleep wouldn't come easily. I didn't want to think about Darrells, the Doctor, or even Maggie. Particularly Maggie.

Surprisingly, I did go to sleep and woke up an hour before arrival time, long enough for an orange juice and a coffee.

Not only was Darrells waiting just outside the customs area of terminal three, but he looked glum as we shook hands. Whatever it was he wanted to talk about weighed on him. You could tell he wanted me to hurry, to move faster, but he didn't say anything. He just set the pace by taking long strides and made a direct line to a black limousine. What the hell is going on? I said to myself. This isn't Darrells' easy though presumptuous style. This big show is a new element. This isn't Darrells.

He opened the door of the car, ushered me in and followed me into the roomy back of the Cadillac. All it needed for clearer identification was a fluttering American flag. A few people turned around to look at us. Once inside, he whispered without any preamble.

"Got your message. Are both Saddam and Barazan still out of Baghdad?"

"Yes, they're both at the front, but should be back any moment. They don't stay long."

"We didn't know how to stop your message from going through as it was because Sue acted on it before I saw it. Maggie would be suspicious. Sue did send roses to Linton with your message unchanged. It was noted on the copy of the telex I read. I hope it's accepted at face value."

"Thanks for telling me. What's this exercise all about?"

"We're going around the corner to the Ballymore Skyline Hotel. There is someone from Washington who wants to meet you. Someone very high up. We'll talk there."

CHAPTER THIRTEEN

The Ballymore Skyline is probably the most characterless hotel in the world. It has a commitment against elegance. Everything is drab and below standard. We moved from corridor to elevator to narrow corridor with Darrells in the lead. He knocked gently on a door which swung fully open to show the patrician figure of a man of about fifty, tall with a receding hairline. He was in a short-sleeve shirt and I recognized the face but couldn't put a name to it. He even moved like an important man.

The long hand which reached to shake mine while holding the door open was skinny, but the handshake was firm and manly.

"Come in, come in. I'm Bill Brandt."

"How do you do, I'm Daoud Al Mousa."

"You must be awfully tired. Thanks for flying over to see us. We arranged for masses of coffee here, croissants and everything a man needs." We both sat down.

"I'm okay, I sleep on planes."

"Well, as Jimmy told you, this won't take long. We might as well get started. Why don't you sit at the other end of the table opposite me? Jimmy will sit in the middle." I obeyed.

God, I have seen better conference rooms. This was a Holiday Inn atmosphere straight out of Boise, Idaho right down to the metal- and plastic-topped tables. But why Brandt? He had made a disaster of negotiating the hostages' release from Iran through Algeria. Some said he single-handedly lost the elections for Jimmy Carter. I thought he was a Democrat and had gone back to a think tank when Reagan got elected, the Mannings Institution or something. Well, they will tell me soon enough. Perhaps he is one of the people who never resign—they just change title.

"Daoud, Bill has something extremely important for us. He wanted to see you in person."

There was a smirk of derision on Darrell's face. Good God, he was human after all. The little Arab boy was moving to the front, outdoing him. Good. What a damn good start to the meeting; I liked the implicit promotion.

At three in the morning my mind stopped wondering long enough to remember that I was in Washington concentrating on the first time I met Brandt at the Heathrow Ballymore Skyline, that I had been doing one of my usual mental reviews. I turned the television set off and drowsily discarded my clothes, but had little difficulty in going back to sleep. Lonely hotel beds are the same everywhere; because they have nothing to offer, they invite thoughts about other times and other places. In this case, exhaustion had almost confused the first meeting which had also included Darrells with the one earlier today. Both had in common that enigmatic sympathetic smile, Brandt's look of compassionate American decency which told me so much and yet nothing. But now I was too tired to think about it or anything else so sleep took over.

I didn't come to until noon and I was thankful for the long, restful sleep which meant I wouldn't have much of a problem wondering what to do in Washington until flight time. I lunched in the hotel dining room, signed the bill and sat uncomfortably in the lobby reading a book about the electronic age written for laymen. I was avoiding my room. Twice I walked outside the hotel's main entrance to listen to the Palestinian gas station operators shouting orders, one time at a poor black guy accusing him of laziness, and I fought a strong urge to cross the street and engage them in friendly conversation, perhaps begging them not to adopt America's prejudices so readily. I wanted to save them the disappointment of discovering the discrepancies between the American dream and the thuggeries of the Butchers of this world, but this thought was interrupted by a tall attractive blond who approached me in the lobby wearing a friendly I-know-who-you-are smile though I didn't recognize her at first, not until I stood up in response to her extended hand.

"Remember me? I'm Cathleen Stranus, DBC News. You were so helpful to us in Baghdad two years ago. You got us an appointment with Dr. Najid."

I thought about how American she was, then answered. "Of course I remember, how are you?"

"Very well. I'm with the Investigative Unit now, with Jerry Dnipe. You know Jerry, don't you? As a matter of fact, he's in London now."

"Of course I know Jerry. How is he?"

"He's fine. He really should see you when you get back there. We're investigating the chemical warfare issue. When do you go back?"

Jokingly I made a sad face. "Leaving tonight."

"Give me your telephone number. He'd love to see you. We need some background on what Iraq and Iran are doing. Nobody seems to know where the chemical plants came from."

The search for a pen in her handbag lasted long enough for me to wonder whether she would be good in bed. What a thought. "I'm not sure I can help, but I'm always happy to talk to Jerry."

"I'll tell him to call you. He's at the Empress Hotel. God, I'd love to talk to you myself, but I've got someone waiting. Jerry will call. It's nice to see you." She rushed off.

My eyes followed her and my friendly thoughts made me smile; it's been a long time. "Very nice to see you and I look forward to hearing from Jerry."

The view from the plane's window was enchanting; it was clear and Washington was beautifully lit and I wondered whether I'd ever return to see the Lincoln Monument again, my favorite Washington landmark. The people in first class looked out of the windows, identified things while making the right comments, arranged and rearranged their pillows, dismantled chair arm rests, unfolded blankets and exchanged seats, all part of the endless ceremony to accommodate two or three hours of sleep.

But sleep wasn't expected and didn't come. I was wide awake hurrying back to Brandt, not the Brandt in Washington, but to our first meeting, back to the ghastly gray Ballymore Skyline Hotel near Heathrow Airport in London. I wanted to continue the examination which I had started on the plane and continued in Washington.

Brandt spoke softly, almost lazily creating his own atmosphere, easily transcending the synthetic surroundings.

"Before we get into Jimmy's brief, how is Baghdad? Do you get any vibes?"

"Okay, the disco at the top of the Mansour Melia is full of dancing boys and girls, rock music and psychedelic lights. I don't wander around—they don't like that. But I don't think there are any shortages. The stores, I'm told, are full of goods. It's a heavy atmosphere. Two colours are prominent in the streets, women in mourning black and men in military uniforms. Saddam's pictures are everywhere—he's the only one smiling. Too damn much, if you ask me. He's on radio, TV and newspapers, opening orphanages, fighting the war, decorating soldiers, talking about the future. He's everywhere. His sex life must be shot to hell. All joking aside, he must be working about a twenty-four hour day. He's got an Indian doctor in residence, but no one knows whether he's sick or if it's just precautionary."

Brandt made haste. "What about the South where the Shias are? Any signs of pro-Khomeini sentiment, any chance of them going to Iran?"

"Too late now," and my hand gesture cut across the distance separating us. "The Iraqi foot soldier is Shia. He fought his Iranian co-religionists and got killed for it. There is blood between them, and that's what matters there. Bill, the basic issue of the war is settled, though Saddam might still lose the battle. Khomeini says religion is supreme and Saddam says the nation state is supreme. On this the Iraqis are with Saddam. That doesn't mean the line might not break somewhere producing an unexpected Iranian victory. That's the big unknown, not the Shias going to Khomeini."

Though he was impressed, he continued. "How is his relationship with his generals?"

"Don't know. Can't broach the subject. I really don't know." I sat back in my chair and played with the ballpoint pen.

"We know he refuses to allow his propaganda machine to mention them by name. They are referred to as Commander Central Sector or First Army or Northern Sector. He doesn't want to allow any of them to become known and liked. Is he that insecure?"

"Don't know. Ask Jimmy." And seeing the unusually silent figure of Darrells, I continued. "He spent seven hours with him, I only saw him for forty-five minutes. I'll tell you something though, the son of a bitch is too tough to be insecure. He oozes it. Khomeini isn't the only one with a sense of mission. Saddam thinks he's Iraq, that he is heaven-sent."

"Jimmy agrees. Let's switch subjects. How are you?"

"Well."

Brandt leaned backwards and became reflective. "I don't want to get personal Daoud, but how are you? We don't like unhappy people on our hands. How is Maggie? That's her name isn't it?"

"She is with her family in Wiltshire. Well, she's unhappy. Doesn't like Americans generally speaking and wants me to quit whatever I'm doing and settle down to making money without complications, a house in the country and a cottage in the south of France."

The touch of human concern followed naturally and was full of sympathy. "You've been together a long time. Why haven't you married?"

"Because I've never asked. I don't think her family would permit a marriage to a person like me, a lowly Arab. You undoubtedly know who they are. And, gentlemen, you don't have anything on them so let's revert to business."

I was being lectured. "I'm sorry Daoud, it wasn't meant to be personal, but we don't want Maggie to know any more than she does, otherwise we should abort this. An unhappy woman is a dangerous one."

"Don't abort anything. She doesn't even want to hear and I won't tell her. She is in Wiltshire, happy with her father's garden, and we are here dealing with a war. She won't do anything to hurt me."

"A dirty, unnecessary war," Brandt mused.

My weariness made me whisper, "Aren't they all, aren't they all."

"Okay Jimmy, you go into the briefing and I will break in when I feel it's necessary."

Darrells pulled out a stack of papers and spread out a map of the Gulf area on the table. He had a ruler which he intended to use as a pointer. The smirk of derision was still there.

"Daoud, the United States Government wants to end the Gulf War. The consequences of its continuing are frightening."

The only interruptions during the two hours which followed were to pour more coffee and answer nature's call. Brandt kept watching me. He did not add to anything Darrells did except to emphasize.

Darrells' finish was out of an executive boardroom. "Any questions, Daoud?"

"No."

"None?"

"Not a single one. I will go back this afternoon. Is my ticket ready and what about a visa?"

The room became deathly quiet and Darrells pulled a folder out of his briefcase. "Here is the ticket. Because you had your passport with you, we issued a new one and Gazzaz stamped a visa in it. He took it upon himself to do this. All Sue had to do was ask. You're all set. Just sign over the picture. Now I'll leave you with Bill. Good luck to you. God damn, I know you will do it."

Our hands clasped firmly. Darrells walked out of the room and Brandt looked at me, stared at the table, then looked at me again.

"Daoud, I understand you have concerns about your future. We would like to put you on a salary."

"No, not a chance. They're paying me. I don't take money from two sides at the same time. As to the future, let's see what happens after this. The future will take care of itself."

Suddenly there was a new crispness in the voice, an attempt to inject a bit of patrician drama. "Why are you doing this? Where is your loyalty?"

"I am doing this for me."

"Tell me more about that."

"It's a long story. When you don't belong, you want what the world denies you—to be a hero. I'm doing this because I think Khomeini is wrong and evil and because I want to do it—for my injured ego. Is that difficult to understand?" For a fleeting moment I wanted to abort, and he felt it.

"I have the feeling that you think you have been cheated, that you are better than the people running things in the Middle East."

I tossed the ballpoint pen up in the air and caught it while deciding that I couldn't back down. "I am. When it comes to that, I'm even better than the people running things in Washington, Bill."

"If it helps at all, I also think you are, but don't be so sensitive about it," he said, though the last part sounded like a warning.

"For Christ's sake, even Darrells didn't like my sudden elevation to dealing with you directly!"

"No, he didn't, I know that." There was a slight pause. "He is worried about Maggie. But I'm not. You want to succeed, which Maggie and Darrells don't understand. You're what we need. Having met you, I know you'll succeed. I also appreciate your refusal to take money. It will serve you well in the future."

"Glad someone understands."

"I must leave. Did you see the shaving kit in the bathroom?

Jimmy arranged it all. Small wonder he doesn't relish his new role. Have a nap, clean up, take the bus to the airport—not a taxi—and go back. We want to hear soon."

"Okay, Bill."

Then he slowly put on his jacket and made ready to go. "Daoud, I am sorry about Maggie. It must be painful. I'm sorry as hell, though I don't know her. I guess most people don't understand the craving of others for personal triumph—even when they're close to them."

When he shook my hand, Bill Brandt looked very much like someone I had known for a while, probably a third or fourth generation Princetonian, a dollar a year man serving the Republic. I couldn't wait to take my clothes off and collapsed on the bed leaving a wake up call with the operator. Darrells, you old bastard. You dirty old bastard. Darrells trying to use Maggie, probably tapping her phone. Oh Maggie, I am beating them my love. I am winning. I am winning, my Maggie. Did you hear me? I am winning, over Darrells and everyone else.

The wake up call from the Ballymore Skyline operator came like the end of a bad dream. I accepted that I was being awakened, but my mind wouldn't accept why or where I was. I had to close my eyes and open them a number of times before final realization of time and place prevailed. I sat on the edge of the bed rubbing my eyes and trying to deal with the unreality of it all.

Enough time for a shower and shave and the bus ride back to Heathrow, the inevitable inspection of the ghastly characterless buildings, the eyesores which people plant next to international airports. Time to make the dream a reality, to live with what was happening to me. Time to continue the journey because it had gone too far to go back on any of it, not with people like Brandt flying to London especially to see me. Even if I had wanted to, I couldn't think of anything else to do. My world was creating itself through sheer momentum.

An hour later I was aboard the same British Airways plane which had brought me from Baghdad. Would the cabin staff be the same? I asked myself. Would one of them approach and identify me? How I wish this could lead to a normal healthy everyday conversation. It would bring me back to earth. I would have to invent a story to justify my long-distance shuttling. What could that be? Selling fire engines. Yes, selling fire engines. Very much in need because of the war. What is wrong with fire engines? A lovely idea. I was pleased with my ingenuity.

The cabin staff were a different collection of British Airways types. The stewards with floating indecisive voices were thin and unmanly. The girls too were a stereotype; chunky blondes with accents considered common by English establishment standards.

There I go again, using my ultra-sensitive antennae to decide whether people belonged or not. Why worry about such things? The first class compartment was almost empty—only three other people. Sleep was a good idea, an easy way out. So why not kick one's shoes off, wrap oneself in the light blanket and close one's eyes until Baghdad. Let's save all thinking until then.

As I suspected, the new passport was a problem; the Iraqi immigration officer didn't like it, nor the visa. He wouldn't admit to having seen me with different ones only two days before. That would be revealing his suspicions. However, he did insist that I see one of his superiors and marched me to a small office occupied by a uniformed army major. The latter had visitors, but had no compunction about interrogating me in their presence, a customary Arab rudeness. I insisted that his visitors leave before submitting to his questioning. Then it was the other way round. I told him I was in Baghdad to see Barazan Hussein, the Chief of Security, that I had been there two days before and my belongings were still at the Mansour Melia Hotel and then pointedly insisted I wasn't ready to answer any questions. The major had a problem on his hands. He called security headquarters, but no one in direct touch with Barazan would speak to him. He stood up militarily and very politely told me that his driver would take me to the Mansour Melia Hotel, but that he'd keep my passport. Brother Barazan's office would return it to me. Initiative won. The problem was solved.

I was delivered to the Mansour Melia looking tired but, given the journey and its contents, in presentable form. I offered a brief Arab salutation to the people at the desk, climbed the marble stairs and went on to my suite. Door shut, I rushed to the phone and dialed Barazan's number. His aide-de-camp was full of excitement. "Where are you? We have been looking all over for you."

"I was out of town. Is Brother Barazan there? Sorry, but I must speak to him immediately. It is a matter of great importance."

"Yes, yes. He wants to speak to you too."

A pause and a click and Barazan was on, loud and happy. "Daoud, where have you been?"

"I had to go to London. I just got back and I must see you."

"Well yes, yes I must see you. But, listen, you must move out of the hotel. We don't want you where you are. Prepare your things and someone will pick you up in half an hour. Move your things then come over here, I will explain when I see you."

I knew when not to question matters. "Okay, see you later."

"Inshallah."

"Inshallah."

Half an hour later, my usual companion was exercising his knock of gentility. I opened the door and there he was. The only difference from old times was the broad smile and a bear hug of an embrace.

"Welcome back, are you ready?"

"Yes, I am."

"Let's go. No need to wait for a porter. I signed the bill. I'll carry the suitcases if you carry your briefcase."

"No, no. I will carry one of them and the briefcase, just help with this one. Let's go."

We walked out of the Mansour Melia without looking left or right, straight to his car. We drove away across one of Baghdad's many bridges along an unfamiliar boulevard. We turned left in front of a tiny building with a crude neon sign with the name Samir Amis. It resembled a pre-oil inn where smelly orientalists stayed to write tales of Eastern romance. He asked me to stay in the car, got out and took my suitcase in. He came back and we drove on.

A protest was in order, but it had to be carefully phrased. "What is that place? A hotel? It didn't look like much. I don't know what this is all about, but I'm not sure I want to stay in that place."

First he shrugged his shoulders, then he decided against being dismissive. "Brother Barazan's instructions. He doesn't want anyone in Baghdad to know you are here. There are foreigners in the major hotels. We don't want your presence known."

"Well, I'll talk to him about it."

"Yes. It's not a bad place. No one important stays there."

The car negotiated narrow streets and kept taking unexpected left and right turns creating the distinct impression that I wasn't to know where we were going. We eventually came to a stop in front of a row of similar houses, small with tiny gardens and little to distinguish them from other Baghdad bungalows. They had the usual white fence and a few citrus trees in front, a rather nondescript entrance next to a wide glass window which looked into the living room. In the case of the one we aimed for, the curtains were drawn, hiding what was inside.

There was a young man standing inside the garden in front of the door. He parted with all informality and stood rigid as my companion turned the knob of the door and entered a totally empty room. My companion walked straight ahead, knocked at a door on the left, entered and saluted. He stepped aside to reveal Barazan sitting behind a large wooden desk underneath a huge smiling portrait of his brother.

He leapt around the desk and hugged me, holding me by the elbows and continued to shake me in his arms.

"Brother Daoud, we were so worried. Thank Allah you are here and safe."

"I am thankful to him to be here, but the airport people should have been able to tell you I left Baghdad."

"They did. They did. But we thought it was an impersonator. Anyway, this is Brother Brigadier Omar and this is Brother Brigadier Hassan. Sit over here close to me. How are you, dear Daoud?"

"I am well, extremely tired but well."

Barazan was fidgety with happiness. "Something exciting must be happening. We'll have coffee."

A bell was rung from a button on the desk, my companion reappeared and coffee was ordered while I avoided the eyes of Omar and Hassan and inspected the room. What a joke. It had been set up for the meeting. A desk, four chairs, Saddam's picture and the Iraqi flag. Nothing else, not a damn thing. Ha, they don't trust me, do they.

"What is up? You come to Baghdad on your own, call me, then call the leader, then go back to London and then come back. What excitement! Tell me!"

"I don't know where to begin. But first things first. The Brother President made it very clear to me that certain matters are to be dealt with strictly between you and me. I have nothing but the utmost respect for Brothers Omar and Hassan. It is true I just met

them—surely my misfortune—however, brotherly goodness
shines from their faces and I personally would trust them with my
life. On the other hand, the word of the Brother President is holy to
me and I must be assured of his approval of everything I do on
matters which affect the nation's destiny." That was a good one,
Daoud, continue, it was well arranged.

Barazan's slurp of his Turkish coffee was louder than usual. He
put the cup down and smiled. "Brother Daoud, the President
himself requested Brothers Omar and Hassan to be with us. We
need the benefit of their wisdom in these difficult days. We keep
no secrets from them. You have the word of the leader himself to
proceed."

"First, allow me to state very clearly how deeply touched I am
that you place so much trust in me. My loyalty is to you. My
American passport can be burnt, but the blood in my veins is pure
Arab. It is true the other side trusts me, but let us make no mistake
about it, Brothers, they are serving their own purposes. Let us then
use this opportunity, but with care and without illusion. For the
time being we have a common enemy, the enemy of Allah,
Khomeini.

"Let us start at the beginning. The Americans have demonstrated their willingness to cooperate with us by giving us the
information about the Russian help to Iran, the satellite pictures."

Barazan nodded approval. "That is indeed true." But Omar and
Hassan stared impassively, hands held across their ample bellies,
as if this was a military gesture. Once Omar moved his hand to his
face to make sure his mustache was there. Sensing victory, I
continued shifting my eyes from one listener to another.

"Now the Americans wish to cooperate with us regarding the
other issue raised by the Brother President, the matter of arms
reaching our enemy. This is a much more complicated matter. It
involves working with the Americans on a continuing basis
because we are talking about the flow of arms, not a single deal.
Though naturally we must start with one deal."

As I paused, Omar's restlessness surfaced. "What about the
spare parts they and their Israeli allies are shipping to our
enemies? Why don't they start there?"

My ready answer was delivered with controlled emotion.
"Because they insist they don't ship any spare parts themselves.
Also they cannot control Begin, but they have told him to stop. I am

146

told the request to him originated in the office of the President of the United States."

Omar threw his hands up in the air in a dramatic gesture of helplessness. "Brother Daoud, the Americans are up to their usual tricks. All they have to do is tell Begin, not request him. He lives off them. Forgive me, but this is nonsense."

"Brother Omar, your words are not strange to me. I hear you well. I am not defending the American position. I am only a messenger acting for us. I am relaying the answer I received. I am not justifying it."

Barazan intervened, stating that the President had requested me to ask the Americans to stop the flow of spare parts to Iran. To Barazan it was obvious the Americans did not want to deal with the issue directly. That would be an admission of guilt on their part. On the other hand he counseled, "Let's see what they told Brother Daoud before we make judgment. It is not a good start—not honest . . . not honest."

I pretended to sigh deeply. "Well, they want to help with everything which reaches Iran from Europe on a deal by deal basis. They claim the CIA knows about most of the European arms deals with Iran. They find out about them very early and can supply us with the information, provided we cooperate with them on the deal. In simple words, Iraqi intelligence and the CIA must work very closely together."

Omar exploded, "It is a diversion. It is a diversion and an attempt to infiltrate us. I am totally against it. Completely out of the question. We want help against our Iranian enemy. We don't want partnership with the Americans. That's treason, working with the CIA."

"Well, I don't know if there is any sense in continuing. I mean this is the basis of their plan and it is being rejected before I fully explain it." My appeal was directed at Barazan, but there was another reaction, a stir where Hassan sat. All eyes turned to him, the silent one. "Brother Daoud," and he clung to the sides of his chair with both hands, "let us not be hasty. Brother Omar meant no harm, I assure you. I need for you to explain the proposed program in full, Brother Daoud. Did they provide you with examples of cooperation, do they have any specific projects in mind?" Hassan had spoken slowly, betraying lack of knowledge as to what had taken place before, but I decided that he was a potential ally.

"Your point is very well taken, Brother Hassan, though working on a selective basis wouldn't make for good relations. Anyway, they have a major proposal which I should like to put to you." I leaned forward, clasped my hands together, looked into their eyes one at a time and proceeded to use my rusty Arabic with unusual precision.

"There are 150,000 rounds of 155mm ammunition ready to be shipped from Italy to Iran. The enemy needs them desperately, they are running short, but you know that. The goods are made by TMIA in Italy at a total cost of about forty-nine million dollars. We've verified the existence of the goods. Some high up TMIA officials are willing to cooperate with us to stop the goods reaching Iran. The Americans told them to cooperate with us and will organize the take out, but they will not pay. The bribe must come from us."

"How much?" snapped Omar.

"Fifteen million dollars."

"But we can't use 155mm!" He was shouting again.

I tried my best to muffle my impatience. "I know. You could give them to Egypt or just blow up or sink the ship. The important thing is to deny it to the Iranians. The TMIA and American people agree with us that no violence should be used. The job will be done after the ship leaves the Italian port. The best thing is to divert it to Egypt. By then the Iranians will have depended on it and will be caught short, as the Americans say, with their pants down."

I laughed and they all joined in and then Barazan took over again. "Daoud, we too have verified this deal. Let's not waste any time on that. But two major things remain, the money is too much. This is Italian banditry. Second, we will not pay until the job is finished."

I explained the scheme of my being held hostage until the job was finished and then authorizing the bank in Lugano to pay. I told them that I was a willing volunteer, that it would expedite the whole operation.

Overwhelming silence encased us. No one could think of anything to say. They gave me furtive glances, looked at each other, shuffled their feet a bit and made unintelligible noises, grunts. They had been challenged, but had nothing to say. Omar stared at the floor, still unhappy.

Hassan came through first. "We do not wish you to be placed in any danger. We value you as a brother. Also it is a bad way to do business. If anything went wrong and the Italians killed you, the whole affair would be exposed." Then, lowering his voice and slapping his thigh with his right hand he continued. "You are our link with the Americans. We do not want the connection exposed. No, it is much too dangerous."

"Well, it is only dangerous if you don't pay."

"Brother Daoud, was this madness your idea? I am sorry, but it is madness," said Hassan with a bit of an edge which he couldn't retract.

"Yes."

"Why?"

"The Italians wanted immediate action, a whole plan. I was there and I am not authorized to do anything except talk. So I offered a way out involving me. It's all I could think of."

Barazan was weighing what to say. "My dearest of brothers, Daoud, the President would not approve. You know thousands of mercenaries offered us their services even for suicide missions. Egyptian frogmen wanted to go in to blow up Kharg Island. A British Air Marshall wanted to teach us how to bomb Tehran. The President always said no. He doesn't like the idea of outsiders fighting our war."

Time to put on a sad face and a sad voice. "I am not a mercenary. I am an Arab trying to do his duty. I'm not doing it for money."

"A million apologies, Brother Daoud. You are the most loyal Arab I know. Perish the thought that you are doing it for money. We just can't have you exposed like that."

"Why not allow me to present my case to the Brother President? There is no time, gentlemen. In three days the ship will be out of Naples. Unless our men are aboard to take over and do what needs to be done, then it's too late. We must immediately agree on two things: how much we are willing to pay and what to do with the cargo. I suggest it goes to Egypt as this would put the Egyptians more solidly on our side. The Americans will do the job."

Barazan was edging forward in his chair. "Brother Daoud, fifteen million dollars is too much. Try five, and if it doesn't work, seven and a half. The goods should go to Egypt. Your reasoning is solid."

"Right. We should offer seven and a half right away and make it a final offer. They'll bite. Then you will inform the Egyptians that we will provide the name of the ship, etc. There is nothing for them to do except receive it and make a fuss through the press to embarrass the Iranians. I will send a telex about the money. When can I see the President? When is our leader free to see me?"

In a minute Barazan was speaking to his brother. "Abu Odei, Brother Daoud Al Mousa is here with us as you know. There is a major problem with what he proposes. He wishes to see you in person to present his point of view and it must be done today or tomorrow. Tonight at eight? Fine, I'll arrange for him to be there."

He turned to me and smiled. "He never sees anyone this fast, Brother Daoud, he must like you. Would you like me there?"

"I would not presume to suggest your absence, but I find it easier when I am alone. I've told you everything and it is up to you and to the leader."

He rang the bell from the desk. "Right, we will have lunch here and then go to have a rest. Your companion will pick you up from the Samir Amis. By the way, sorry about that, but it's much more discreet than the Mansour Melia. There are all types of exiles in the Mansour Melia whose loyalty we have yet to verify, people from other parts of our great Arab nation, ones we don't know well . . . and spies posing as foreign correspondents."

Food was brought in. Someone told a joke and we each had our turn and the laughter was loud even when not justified. There was lots of rice-based food, lots of slapping on the back and shaking of the hands when the story was funny. We finished by four in the afternoon and my companions drove me away after I received kisses on both cheeks from Barazan, Hassan and Omar. This gesture of affection normally reserved for hellos and good-byes emphasized the importance of the occasion. Back to the remarkably bare hotel room. A single bed with a lamp that went off and on by itself, a round table, two locally made chairs, and a radio which emitted static, providers of eternal discomfort for the lower classes. I was totally annoyed, but there might be something to keeping a low profile. I doubt whether anyone would have found me at the Samir Amis.

I hung my clothes up on wire hangers and threw myself on the bed, still extremely annoyed at being in the shabby hotel, but I fell asleep until six. I then got up and managed to use the trickle from the shower to clean and went downstairs looking for a bar. There it was: a Western saloon full of expatriate workers drinking beer from cans. What a dive. Except for the multiplicity of languages, it could have been out of a Western. I didn't mind the people, but the place was dirty. Still, perhaps they could manage a vodka and soda. The barman did, but with a look which queried the combination. I had two large ones, unwise but enough to relax me for my meeting, then I suddenly remembered that I hadn't telexed London. The combination of tiredness and utter involvement had left me in a foggy state of mind.

I made a dash to the hotel's front desk and inquired whether they had a telex machine. Allah was with me—they did.

> 22335 ONWARD (LONDON)
> ATTENTION: SUE
> PLEASE CONTACT DARRELLS AT DORCHESTER MOST
> URGENTLY. PREFERABLY CARRY COPY OF THIS AND
> LEAVE FOR HIM THERE. HE IS TO ADVISE MEAT MAN
> ITALIAN GOODS OKAY FOR HALF PRICE ASKED. BUYER IS
> EGYPT AND OFFER IS FINAL.
> PLEASE CALL MAGGIE, LINTON, WILTSHIRE, AND TELL
> HER SHE IS MISSED.
> CHEERS,
> DAOUD.

My companion arrived as I was giving the desk clerk the telex and explaining the urgency of it. The desk clerk recognized the intruder and nodded, then promised to transmit the telex immediately. We walked out of the Samir Amis and turned right to the parked black car. Our routine in reaching the presidential palace was easier than the last time; obviously someone had been alerted and instead of methodical searches there were piercing looks inside the car to determine who the important occupants were and then the motion to continue.

The Colonel was at the door. It was two minutes before eight. We followed the same procedure, even down to the knocking and entering without waiting. Saddam Hussein rose, took off his glasses and this time moved sideways then half a step forward. The Colonel stepped aside and I moved with a long stride and bowed. "Brother President." His hands held my shoulders to lift me and look into my eyes and then he kissed me on both cheeks.

"Brother Daoud, welcome, welcome home, welcome to Baghdad."

"It is nice to be home, Brother President."

"Sit down. Right where you were last time. Coffee will be here soon. You look well, considering all your travels. Even Milan, I long to go there too, to Northern Italy, if ever time will allow."

In reality he looked a bit tired and not as soldierly as the first time I had met him. He smiled. "Soon I hope, Brother President. Soon this evil war will be over and you can go there to rest. Though if you will allow me, you look in perfect shape."

"Thank you, Daoud. Thank you. Now Daoud, Brother Barazan was here most of the afternoon. He briefed me. What is this all about? Tell me."

"Brother President, we have an exceptional opportunity to damage the enemy. I don't mind risking my life. There are other ways, but it would take time to arrange them and we don't have the luxury of time. We need to act."

"I will get back to that specific problem later. I am more interested in America's sudden willingness to cooperate with us. Why? True, we made specific requests, but they didn't go as far as overall cooperation. This deal on the 155s—I understand there will be others?"

"Certainly, the Libyans are negotiating a bigger arms deal with Austria on behalf of Iran—a company called Hanbinger. All types of material, about $165 millions' worth. Then there is an order for 203mm stuff from Spain. This one, as you know sir, is vital. The 203 is the only gun which can penetrate your fortifications. There are many others. They—the Americans—know everything going on in this area."

He became angry. "Son of a dog Kreisky. He's like a wandering whore. Whoever is there first, whoever pays—even Qaddafi. Nonetheless, the Americans want to go for that one as well. I guess there will be more, and each time there is a new one they learn more about us and our ways. What do you think, Daoud? You know them. I don't trust them, do you?"

"Mr. President—"

"Brother President, Daoud. I am only Mr. President to those who don't know me."

I responded to his invitation with a smile of thanks. "Brother President, I think the time has come to tell you the most important news I have. I withheld something from Brothers Barazan, Omar and Hassan. That is why I was desperate to see you. I used the matter of being held hostage as a way, as an excuse. If it hadn't worked, I would have tried something else. I gave the Americans an undertaking that this matter would be discussed with you alone."

"Darrells—quite a character. We have a full file on him all the way to Beirut days. Anyway, what is he up to now?"

"Brother President, this isn't from Darrells. This is from Bill Brandt who is very close to McClane, Reagan's foreign policy man."

"You say Brandt?"

"Yes. That's why I flew back to London. He came to see me."

"Brandt came to London especially to see you! What did he want?"

"Your cooperation, Brother President. He wants your cooperation in overthrowing Khomeini, the enemy of Allah."

"Continue, don't stop until the end." The initial surprise evaporated and he was back in command.

"Brandt told me that the US is in direct contact with high ranking elements in the Iranian Air Force. They were all US trained and the US took the precaution of recruiting some of them under the Shah, just in case. Some of these fellows have now been promoted to positions of power, the old upper command having been executed or fled the country. They believe, the Iranian Air Force people, that Khomeini can be neutralized. They don't want to kill or depose him—too difficult. They want to reduce him to a figurehead by destroying his power base, the clergy and the Moslem Youth, and then isolate him.

"Their plan is to use some commando units, round up the mullahs and execute them summarily, bomb the two major camps of Moslem Youth, surround Khomeini's residence and cut him off from the rest of the country after announcing he is alive and still head of state. Some think he adores power so much he'd cooperate with anyone to stay on top."

"Daoud, Daoud, Daoud. Naive nonsense. What about the army, the foot soldiers who will occupy the street? If you don't have foot soldiers, you have nothing. You can't overthrow a government this way. The Americans are hopeless." His hands went up in the air.

"Brother President, America will always be naive. But we have nothing to lose." My plea was subdued to avoid taking too American a position.

"I don't know. What do they want from Iraq? We can't allow them to recruit our people while they pretend to help us." There was a flicker of a knowing smile on Saddam's face.

"They want you to announce a unilateral truce the moment the move against Khomeini is made. No army can go against its own government while it's threatened from outside. This absolves them from any sense of guilt."

"Can't do that. It would look like collusion and it would destroy the anti-Khomeini forces—some of them are our friends. But if we declare a truce before the Air Force moves, stating that we will only shoot in self-defense and saying we hope the other side will see the wisdom of bringing an end to bloodshed and respond accordingly, then maybe it will look like an accident."

"That is most sound, Brother President. I'm sure they will accept it. I don't care if the whole thing fails, it will still weaken Khomeini. One other thing, sir, a declaration renouncing territorial claims on Iran must also be made at the same time."

"We never had any so there is no problem with that. When is all of this supposed to happen?"

"In two weeks."

"Will you pass on my comments to Brandt and contact me confirming his acceptance of my suggestion? It's the only way."

"Yes, Brother President. Also, sir, we must forget the other deals for now. I can't do this while I am hostage. So it is best if the brothers are told that you turned my request down. I will see if Brandt can get the Egyptians to intercept the ship anyway, without us."

"Yes, yes. No field cooperation with America."

"Furthermore, sir, Brandt says this must remain between us."

"There are a lot of secrets between us, Daoud. Even that poor professor you and Darrells blackmailed into working for the CIA back in the late sixties." It sounded like a weary refrain.

"Brother President, I was working against Russia."

"Of course, Daoud, of course, Radio Freedom. He teaches here now. Highly thought of. Managed to come to see me after seeing you in the lobby of the Mansour Melia."

"Oh! that explains the Samir Amis."

"Telephone me in a week. Take the new number. Let's say exactly in one week at six, Baghdad time. If you fail, the following day same time. Our code name for Brandt is Skunk, okay?" He didn't give me time to react; he had moved behind his desk and made a notation in his diary and gave me a tiny piece of paper with a number on it.

"Mr. President, you have been most generous with your time. Thank you."

"Come back to see me soon. Do you play chess, Daoud?"

"Yes, Brother President."

"We'll have a game one day. I bet you're good."

"No, I'm not. Don't have the patience—I become emotional."

"We'll see. Good-bye Daoud. And please call me Brother Saddam."

"I am more than honored, Brother Saddam."

Another exit routine and more ranting, repetitive reflections. To the Samir Amis this time, and the ghastly airport, no time for niceties and long Arab good-byes. My companion would tell Barazan I went back to London. I told him to do so. I also asked him to arrange my seat on the plane. There was forty-five minutes left before departure. Perhaps there was a way of delaying it without too much fuss.

It took me five mad minutes to pack and rejoin my companion in the lobby as he was paying my bill in cash. My suitcases were rushed to the car without anything being said. When he finally moved off, I asked him if he had made all the arrangements.

"No, but I did call headquarters and asked them to delay the plane. Brother Barazan was told. If there are no seats, we will get one of the regular passengers off. That's not a problem."

He drove through Baghdad as if it were any empty desert road with little or no regard for pedestrians, donkeys or stray animals. His long arms manipulated the steering wheel with agility. He enjoyed the sound of screeching tires and showing off his mastery of the vehicle and his panache. Unconsciously, he was advertising the importance of his mission and I was envious of his enjoyment of what he did.

We came to an unsteady stop in front of Saddam International.

A porter was commanded to put my things aboard the plane directly. My companion went to the desk past a queue of about twenty waiting passengers and reappeared with a boarding ticket. He walked me over to the boarding gate. "Allah be with you. Brother Barazan told me to get you to the plane no matter what. Have a safe journey and see you soon." For reasons unknown to me his eyes watered. He warmly kissed me on both cheeks.

I walked through the tube, the people conveyor, aboard the 747 past a collection of curious eyes both admiring and fearful of the cause of their delay. They seemed to be asking who I was. It was the right question.

The familiar roar of engines and slow turning round. The uncertain halting move towards a runway, the grunting of the core of the plane ready to unleash its heavy self upon the tarmac and then the eventual lift-off. All in five minutes, all as fresh and intriguing as the first time. If someone would only explain it to me in layman's language, perhaps the sense of total disbelief would go away: how does a plane become airborne, how does it stay up there?

The now familiar emptiness of the first class cabin—four people this time. The total darkness. Saddam, Barazan, Brandt, the old history teacher from Beirut days, the intricacy of the situation. Maggie everywhere, every moment. Maggie in Cairo, Kuwait, Amman and Bahrain. Maggie in St. Malo, Maggie in Haiti. Maggie funny in unfeminine woolen socks during a cold February insisting on wearing the socks to bed. Further back, Bethany stories and all the laughter. Father Theodesios making wine and sharing it with an unaccustomed Bethany people and the innocent mischief it all created and Maggie's twinkling eyes asking for more. Maggie becoming everything in my life, giving it meaning, an anchor, the home I never had.

Come on Daoud, come on baby. You're tough. You're tough or you wouldn't be in the middle of all this. The doubts, questions, stay within. No one ever sees that. No one suspects it—except Maggie perhaps. She knows you, your background, the chip on the shoulder, the craving to reach the top—even through the so-called back door.

God damn it to hell. I don't know which is the footnote to which. Is life sleeping in planes, the tantalizingly and extremely dangerous telephone calls and bad paperbacks, the preludes to the journey into torment, the mission to satisfy the thirst for recognition? Or is it the other way round? A home with Maggie, perhaps kids. Are plane sleep, criminal telephone conversations and paperbacks much more natural in the end? Better not confuse them. But to go from a bad paperback, then sleep and then London and then Brandt and then Darrells and then the office and then Maggie. I'm not sure about the order of things any more. Time to sleep. Yes, time to rest the weary, overworked head.

For a reason I cannot explain until now, I believe that I started dreaming before I fell asleep—if that is possible. It was a long, vivid happening, perhaps what people call a nightmare.

In my dream it was summer and the sun was bright and warm in a totally unEnglish way. I was wearing a pair of swimming trunks and slippers, wandering around the South Audley Street patio picking up dead leaves and checking on the flower pots. Suddenly, for no explainable reason, I lost my balance and stepped on an unguarded skylight which shattered under my foot and I was sucked in, falling through another layer of glass on top of the landing, but managing to stay on my feet.

I remember small bits of glass falling all around me as if in a slow motion scene from a film, and I remember that I landed with a heavy thud, looked at my uninjured hands and moved forwards towards the door which led upstairs back to the office only to see Michael running down towards me three and four steps at a time. I was totally dazed and Michael asked whether I was alright and instinctively I put my left hand behind me and told Michael that I had a wedge of glass in my back. It was wedged in my back the way movie knives stick in the backs of actors. Michael helped me to sit down and instructed me to keep talking to avoid passing out and I remember looking at Michael and saying, "Tell Maggie I love her. What a silly way to go. What a silly way to go."

The dream continued in minute details covering surgery and a stream of visitors including Maggie, who came to see me only one time to inform me that I looked well and that the doctor told her it was only a matter of time. She therefore felt free to go visit a chinaware factory somewhere in the North. Maggie disappeared North never to appear again and recuperation took place at home under the care of a nurse. Though it took a long time, everything was going according to the medical plan.

The end of the dream was in my doctor's small office in Sloane Street with both of us somber, finding it very difficult to communicate. That's when the doctor announced to me that I had suffered "a severe shock to the system which resulted in impotency—in all likelihood, temporary." The dream drew to its conclusion with me thanking God Maggie was gone and rushing home to place a telephone call to my brother Raouf to ask him to come to see me. I needed to tell someone what had happened to me and Raouf was the one I trusted most with my disturbing problem, the one who would understand and whose understanding would ease the pain. Yes, Raouf.

Raouf and I loved each other. Years before, early in his revolutionary career, Raouf had chosen me as legatee. He had talked to me about what he was doing and concluded his short statement by asking me whether I would accept "the trust" and I had accepted. The slogan of his group was "If I Fall Take My Place" and he wanted me to take his place if anything happened to him. Yes, it has to be Raouf.

I woke up before the dream telephone call to Raouf was made, looking at my fellow passengers and wondering whether I had spoken in my sleep, whether I had tossed and turned or made painful sounds. I was anxious to determine whether I had given away anything. If they had noticed anything they didn't seem to care. In fact, they paid no attention whatsoever, a strange source of disappointment.

Nobody was at Heathrow to meet me this time. A simple black taxi to South Audley Street. A slight drizzle, empty 7:00 a.m. streets and a cabbie who ceased his chatter only after a valiant try. He stopped only when told sir had only been away for two days, so there was no need for a full brief on life in London. He was overtipped to compensate for his sensitivity.

A cumbersome climb up the stairs past the office area, past the landing, the site of my dream accident. I left the suitcases on the first floor in front of the offices so that all would know I had returned and climbed the last stretch of the stairs to greet Ecstasy and Blacks. They occupied their usual spot, the top of the stairs. I patted both and turned into the kitchen to look at their food plates. Maggie wasn't back. It was Sue alright; more dry food than wet. They differed on what was good for the innocent animals. That established, I went into the bedroom with the cats in pursuit. They were saying they had missed me. This time I didn't tell them that I missed them too. I went to sleep. Pure heavy sleep full of fatigue. It was like going away, like taking leave.

I was awakened by the familiar voice of Michael who was sitting on the edge of the bed reluctantly shaking me by the shoulder. I looked at him vacantly.

"What time is it Mike?"

"It's three in the afternoon. Jimmy Darrells is on the phone. He called before, but I didn't want to disturb you. Do you want to talk to him?"

"Yes. I'll plug this phone in. Hang up when I get on."

"Okay." He ran downstairs.

"Daoud, you're exhausted — well, understandably."

"What's up?"

"Nothing, we want to see you. Bill is still here."

I gulped. "Dorchester?"

"Afraid not. 69 Ennismore Gardens, a mews house. Do you know where it is?"

"Yes, near where I drink."

"Yes, I know. How about six?"

"Okay."

"See you then."

I rolled back and tried to go back to sleep. No chance. Right, let's use the evil instrument. I dialed Maggie. There it was, her thin crisp voice.

"Hello."

"It's me."

"Oh. When did you come back?"

"This morning."

"How is funland?"

"Can't I get any rest?" I pretended to yawn.

"Not when you send flowers with messages which upset my parents."

"What's that?"

"They thought you wanted them to be out of our lives."

"Camel shit. It had nothing to do with that."

"What did it have to do with then? It was nothing to do with me I bet."

"Well the flowers were for you."

159

My attempt to make light of things didn't work. "What about the rest?"

"I love you."

"Try again."

"I still love you, believe me."

"Don't beg. I don't like it."

"I'm not begging, I'm making a statement of fact."

"Was that a coded message?"

"Which one?"

"I'll hang up."

"Yes it was, but the roses were for you. Maggie, I missed you, believe me."

"I am secondary. I just do what you want. Glory is what matters."

"What? You know you're hardly that. Why not Gavroche it tonight?"

"Blood money."

"Stop it. Please stop it." I wasn't angry.

"Okay—when?"

"Nine. Meet you there. Can't do it before."

"I told you I'm secondary."

"And I told you I love you and missed you every moment. God, did I miss you."

"See you at nine."

"Do you love me?"

"Sometimes."

"Do you love me?"

"I said sometimes."

"See you at nine."

"Alright then."

I made an attempt at making myself presentable and went downstairs full of relief because everything around me was normal, happy and easy and had none of the energy-sapping tension of the immediate past. I thanked Sue for taking care of the cats and then had a brief chat with Mike and Martin to tell them Iraqi business was going to increase. I said it was still confidential, but that we should expect a major PR assignment covering all of Europe. I admitted much of it would be farmed out to other PR firms, but we would control the budget and make lots of money out of it. Both of them were pleased, though they wanted to know more about the new assignment and what brought it about.

There were bills to be paid, everyday letters to be answered and copies of reports from Mike and Martin on their efforts to deal with the world during my absence. Nothing important, but good enough to bring me to a quarter to six and a taxi to Ennismore Gardens and Darrells and Brandt.

CHAPTER FOURTEEN

The stewardess, tiptoeing along the aisle of the Washington to London flight to check on her passengers and expecting them to be asleep, was surprised to find me sitting up staring at nothing in particular. She leaned over to inquire whether I needed anything and became aware that I was being kept awake by unhappy thoughts. She moved away in an apologetic American way to rejoin her colleagues in the service compartment of the plane.

In a moment I was back to three months ago and Darrells and Brandt and the place in Ennismore Gardens in the heart of London, someone's living room, wedding pictures of a smiling couple, silver-framed pictures of a distinguished looking bearded man which went back to the early part of the century and silver gadgets everywhere, covering three tables and an antique desk. All suggested money, probably the house of the local CIA station chief, but who cares.

Brandt was his matter-of-fact self and both greeted me in a relaxed fashion.

"Sit over there, Daoud. Exhausted?" asked Brandt.

"Bone weary."

"Like a drink?"

"Yes please, vodka and soda."

"Vodka and what?" chimed Darrells. "This is a new one on me."

"Vodka and soda. Healthy and pure."

"Well Jimmy, you're being educated in your new job. Can you fix one of them for Daoud?"

A vodka and soda appeared. Darrells poured himself a bourbon on the rocks, but Brandt declined to indulge.

"Well, Daoud. Tell." Brandt smiled.

"He is with us."

"You did it! Son of a bitch," Darrells exclaimed, trying to get in the middle of things.

"Wait, wait. He doesn't want it to appear like collusion. We must signal him and he'll announce a unilateral truce for the sake of peace, four days or so ahead of any internal Iranian move. I convinced him he's ahead no matter what happens."

"Well done. What else?"

"Nothing else. No cooperation on anything else. They don't trust us. Also Mr. Darrells, they know about us and Beirut. The professor we got fourteen years ago is there and he spilled the beans. The guy from Beit Rafafa. So, I'm cooked."

Brandt looked at me. "They're better than we thought. Were you in danger?"

"Don't know. One is in danger just by being in the bloody country. What difference does it make?"

"All the difference in the world. You were speaking for the US Government."

"Yeah, yeah, an instant on the spot foreign policy maker."

Brandt raised a hand in a gesture for me to stop. "That deserves more than yeah, yeah, Daoud. I mean it and wish you'd make your mind up between being a frustrated hippie or one of us. Sorry Daoud, I know you're tired, but so are we."

"Whatever I am, I am not one of you."

"Why?"

"Because." I put my cigarette out.

"That doesn't say anything."

"If it did, I wouldn't have said it."

"I can see you're overwrought, but that's to be expected. We'll talk about it another time. Did you deal with him alone?"

"Yes, we were all by our cosy selves."

I told Darrells and Brandt what had happened. I told them every detail I could remember. Brandt's only comment was, "Well, you are on a first name basis now. Can't do better than that. But Daoud, control the flippancy. You're taut. You couldn't have done better."

"I can do better now. I can go to Le Gavroche where Maggie is waiting."

"Well, you better go now if she's waiting. Stay put—we'll be in touch." Brandt was unhappy.

Maggie was already at the table. I leaned over and kissed her on the lips and she actually smiled in a natural way I hadn't seen for a while. I sat on a chair next to her at a table with four places.

"How's wese?"

"Wese okay. How's the goon squad?"

"The same."

"Delighted."

"Are you sure?"

"No—disgusted." But it wasn't meant to be serious.

"I am pleased to see you."

"Cut that out. Not your style."

"I really am."

"And I am you, but as long as I live I will never know why this had to happen, why you are doing this."

We ordered two vodkas and sodas and tried to divert the conversation to all of the paperbacks I had read. I mentioned *A Candle for a Dark Journey* and she laughed and thought I had invented the title and I had to assure her that I hadn't. I described the nonstop show at the Khan Marjan and a drunken local who had wandered around the tables kissing the hell out of everyone until he reached our table, saw Barazan and sobered up on the spot. She laughed. We ordered dinner—gazpacho, pheasant and a bottle of St. Emilion. I asked about Wiltshire and got a flowery answer about how nice it was, about how pleased her parents were to see her for such a long time and how much she preferred the countryside to cities. It was like old times with all the freshness of liking what we said to each other, without any trace of unease or rejection.

I held her hand and looked at her and all the pain and doubt fled from my mind. Oh, my dear, my own Maggie. Just one more week. Triumph is just around the corner and then I will be putty in your hands.

It was a beautiful summer night and we walked from Le Gavroche to South Audley Street and I was feeling my drink and singing American college songs while she stayed a step or two behind, watching me with gentle amusement. I could tell how pleased she was to see me, but when we passed Grosvenor Square I playfully suggested we make love in the middle of the trees and she giggled and pointed to the US Embassy across the street and said that whoever operated the spy cameras would love to catch us in the act. Yet damn it, that evening I did manage to transmit uncomplicated love to her and it pleased her and brought a glitter to her face. We climbed the stairs to my flat, said a word or two to Ecstasy and Blacks and went to bed. I turned around on my right side and put out my left arm to bring her towards me, but there was no response.

"Maggie what's up?"

"I don't feel like it."

"But I thought everything was alright."

"That's what I thought. It just isn't though."

"What is it?"

"You know, I really can't cope with what you are doing. It turns me off. The whole thing is unnecessary, this craving to be in front. What does it matter? Why? Even when it made me unhappy, you didn't seem to care. It's like pursuing a claim. I can't explain it—it's in you."

Christ, I dreaded those moments, but this time I was determined to try to explain and I told her that it was to defeat the Darrells of this world. The substitute for the invitation from her parents to meet me, the one which never came . . . so many years of waiting for it. "All joking aside, Maggie, did you know that I wanted to marry you? but didn't dare ask because I was afraid of your parents, even before you spoke of their wealth and their attitude."

My explanation didn't work. As a matter of fact it backfired.

"You fool, Daoud. You fool. If only you had asked when we first met. Even last year. I so wanted to marry you then. I wanted you, not your sense of self-importance. And I didn't give a damn about what my parents thought. I never dared bring any of my clothes here except two skirts and some knickers. Thought you'd object."

"Is it too late now?"

"Yes, you've changed. You're back chasing the shadows of Kim Philby and Richard Sorge. It's a dirty business—I can't help it. I think it is the filthiest business there is. Spying on friends and colleagues, resorting to trickery and disguise. Let's just go to sleep if we can."

"What the hell are you on about now?" I shouted.

"About your filthy business, about you!"

"And what the fuck is that supposed to mean?"

When she didn't answer, I pulled the duvet off the bed violently. "Listen lady, I'm talking to you. What the fuck is that supposed to mean? I want a clear answer, are you going to stop this shit or not? I've had it, all you bastards think about is your rose gardens. The holier than thou shit has got to stop. Christ, resorting to trickery and disguise. For your information what I'm doing is not only important, it is necessary and I don't give a damn about what the world thinks about it. I really don't give a big shit what the world thinks, okay? I am what I am. If you don't like that, then piss off." I had pounded the bed with my fist and she sat there staring at me as if I had gone mad, wide-eyed, frightened and silent. I wished I hadn't said anything, particularly about people who write letters to *The Times*, but I couldn't take any of it back and didn't try. Eventually I jumped out of bed and put the duvet back where it belonged while she gave me an unmistakable look of fear. I turned the light off and settled for "We seem to run around in unhappy circles."

A restless night, but I didn't toss and turn because I didn't want her to know how I felt. She too was awake. In the morning we had a silent cup of coffee at the Campanina after which she left saying nothing and I returned to everyday work.

There were no communications from Brandt for two days. I didn't even know whether he and Darrells were still in London. I was tempted to establish contact, but decided against it. They knew I was there.

Routine work occupied my time. I saw Maggie every night and she repeated herself with annoying clarity, though in a gentle way which didn't cause argument. The waiting wasn't bad. I needed a rest. On the fifth day, Darrells phoned.

"He wants to see you today. Same place, same time."

"Okay, see you then."

I was there at six in the evening. I don't know whether it is hindsight or what, but something was wrong. Three days was too long. Then there was that dullness in Darrells' voice. None of the sparkle of expectation.

Sure the setting was the same with Darrells opening the door and Brandt occupying the middle of the room, but the atmosphere was different. A round of hand shaking and I sat down opposite Brandt. They didn't offer me a drink or indulge in any preliminaries.

"Daoud, do you read the *International Herald Tribune*?" Asked Brandt in the manner of a schoolmaster addressing a naughty pupil.

"Yes sir, every day."

"Did you see anything strange today?"

"No, nothing that registered."

He handed me a *Herald Tribune* open at page three with a circle around a small item. The headline read "Iran Said to Hold Anti-Khomeini Plotters". The story was datelined Beirut and it said that the five people arrested were high ranking Air Force officers.

I collapsed backwards in my chair and looked at Brandt. "Our boys?"

"Yes, they were."

"Fucking hell! He won't believe it, he'll think we misled him again. Jesus Christ himself."

Anger, controlled, coherent anger, surfaced in a now pacing Bill Brandt. "He'll have to believe it. We'll make him God damn believe it because he is responsible for this. First we want you to go to see him tomorrow and this is what you'll tell the prick from Takreet, the wonderful guy who helped establish Khomeini's Islamic crap by starting the Gulf War. . . ."

Two hours later I was home repacking my suitcase, feeling like all the international salesmen I so despised. I called Maggie, told her of my plan and suggested it was a bad idea for us to meet, but I wanted her to remind me about the dream next time we met. I was too tense, too preoccupied. She was calm. She knew I was in no mood to discuss or argue. She remotely wished me a good trip and hung up—not a word to ask about the dream.

I got up at six in the morning and dialed Saddam Hussein's private number. He answered the phone in person.

"Brother Saddam, sorry to bother you, but I will be on today's plane to Baghdad. May I see you tomorrow, sir? It is most important."

"Naturally. They will bring you in to see me at 10:00 a.m. It will give you a few hours to rest."

"Look forward to seeing you, Brother Saddam."

"Yes Daoud. You'll be welcome." The absence of enthusiasm was noticeable.

The same agonizing routine and nagging thoughts, variations on an ugly theme. What a stupid, unreal, Mickey Mouse world, as Maggie said. What lunacy. No sleep, not a wink. No reading. Just aimless mental wandering. Six long hours of it. Yes Maggie, there must be a better way to live. It seems to come easier to people with roots, people who can enjoy life as a continuity and not as a drama. That's what you gave me, a base, but not enough. I couldn't have you all the way, at least that's what I thought. The fears of settled people like your parents intruded. They don't like wanderers. Oh well, that's history now.

The repeat performance continued. My companion was waiting with his kiss of greeting. To the Mansour Melia this time. Why the change back I will never know. I was to be picked up in time for the appointment with Saddam.

Still no sleep in spite of a refreshing shower and shave. I'll wait, damn it. I will just wait. There was nothing else to do.

The third visit to Saddam's palace was even easier than the second. Gates were swung open all the way. The Colonel was there waiting, leading me to Saddam's office in the exact, unimaginative fashion of the previous two times.

Saddam didn't budge from behind the desk. I had to walk over all the way. We shook hands. It was clear he didn't want to be kissed. Our glumness precluded the usual niceties.

"Sit down, Daoud. The usual place. But speak up. You have a tendency to whisper."

"Mr. President, the operation is over. The Air Force people in Iran have been arrested. This is definite. We have good reason to believe they were executed."

"I know. We heard. We are not as remote from happenings within Iran as you think. But we don't know why. Did your people turn them in? Did someone in Washington think a weak Iran would invite Soviet intervention or did they think the government there is right wing and close to their hearts? What happened?"

"Mr. President, my brother . . . no. There was no change of heart in Washington. There was a leak from here, from Baghdad, from your Cabinet."

"Careful, Daoud. My colleagues are fellow strugglers, members of the party. Why would they? Why would anyone here do anything to help Khomeini?"

"Mr. President, did you inform your Cabinet?"

"Yes."

"The information was transmitted to Iran from your Foreign Ministry via Athens. As far as we know, it was done on the instructions of your Foreign Minister. A messenger delivered a message by hand to an Armenian who works for you in Greece, Haig Malasian, with instructions to deliver it to the Iranians the same day. Malasian did as he was told. There is no way to tell whether he knew what he was doing."

He sat there immobile. He was devastated. He shrank in size. All sparkle left his eyes. There was cold anger in him. All the outside charm took leave. Suddenly I saw the killer in him and he frightened me. The weakness of his Government was exposed and Saddam wasn't the type of man to like that. He wouldn't even discuss it.

"Mr. President, the Iranians put two and two together, determined who the Air Force officers were and here we are."

"My most trusted colleague, Dr. Madoun Saddeh. He did not approve of our flirtation with you. I say with you, I mean America. He was dead set against it. Thought that we could manage without America's help and that we should eventually join forces with Iran against Israel. Well, well. . . ."

"Mr. President, my friends in London have a suggestion to make. Saddeh shouldn't be punished or exiled. There should be no noise, otherwise it would be seen as weakness by the outside world. He should be allowed to resign. We know he doesn't want Iran to win, but he is opposed to the US in principle and we also don't want that to come out. That's okay. But it should be an easing out process rather than something more drastic."

"Daoud, will you be visiting us again?" he said as he rose.

"No, Mr. President. There is no need for me any more. Besides, I need more time with my family in London."

"How much of a family do you have?"

"Maggie my wife and Ecstasy and Blacks, the two cats." Saddam smiled just a tiny bit. "Good-bye Daoud. Safe journey home tonight."

We shook hands. For reasons I can't explain I wanted to plead for Saddeh, but found it impossible since I had never met him. It would have been out of order, interference in their internal affairs. I had said enough.

The Colonel and I marched down towards the elevator. Saddam wanted me out of the country immediately, tonight. The Colonel made side glances at me. He knew something had gone wrong. Again, there was a cold good-bye.

As my companion drove away, I knew I'd never see Saddam

again, never call him brother again. It was over. It was lost. The last cry for recognition had failed. I couldn't help it; it came out like a moan: "Oh Maggie, you better be there when I return. You'd just better be there."

My companion stared at me as if I had gone mad. He had good reason.

CHAPTER FIFTEEN

The trip back from Baghdad was occupied with what would happen to Madoun Saddeh, the man of principle who had torpedoed our plans and with them my footnote to history, then the inevitable wondering about Maggie and how to mend things. I was desperate to tell her about Saddeh, the man who had brought my foolish dreams to naught.

Only Maggie would understand how alone I was, I told myself. Only she knew how much it all meant to me. The real stuff was Maggie and what we had, not the dreams of would-be heroes, but I needed her to tell me that again. I had begged for Maggie to be there, to take me away from it all, to include me in her reality away from the search for empty glory.

I had called and asked for my colleague Mike to pick me up. Mike sounded strange, but then perhaps it was because I seldom wanted to be met. Little did he know.

Mike winced at seeing me. I must have looked tired, horrible. He carried my suitcases to his car and we headed towards London. He didn't know what to say and I didn't want to say anything.

Suddenly, instinctively, I put my index finger in my mouth and bit into it as hard as I could, just the way I had as a child when I had done something wrong. It hurt like hell and that's what I wanted.

"Michael, is Maggie gone?"

"Yes, I am afraid she has. That's what I wanted to tell you on the phone. She moved her things from upstairs yesterday—mostly books. I helped her move them."

"Did she take Blacks with her—her black cat?"

"Yes, she did."

"Little Blacks too. Then it's for real. Do you know where she is?"

"I hate to tell you this, but she moved to Sam Braill's place."

I looked at him. I wanted reconfirmation of what he had said, but he was looking straight ahead at the road.

"Sam Braill? Jesus Christ, not him. He's an idiot, a fifty-five year old public school kid, stutters and stammers and tells stories that have no end. Starts every sentence with 'I'm sorry'. Christ, he's a sweaty boiled egg. Oh God, mercy. She is so desperate to make a point. Only a desperate person would go for Braill. God, if she has gone this far then there is no turning back."

I undid the safety belt and put my head between my knees and sobbed, "No Maggie—Braill, oh God help me."

Nothing was normal after that; nothing mattered. Brandt and Darrells were told of the meeting with Saddam. They had nothing to say. They kept waiting for me to ask them to live up to their promises to me for if things failed, but I wasn't interested. We settled for a middle class promise to stay in touch. Michael and Martin were given two months to find jobs; their protests were muffled by the fact that they were invited to take some of the business with them. Friends and acquaintances were avoided. I began creating a state of siege around myself, the coffee shop, the pub, the drinking got worse after the empty telephone calls started, and the cry for help to Anna—which became inevitable after pride stood in the way of reconciliation with Maggie.

Lovely Anna wanted to know about what happened with Maggie. Well, well . . . I can't do that, Anna. Braill rankles to this day though Maggie, I was told, left him after a boring two months. Braill is a joke in bad taste because no one is that uninteresting, that accommodating and subservient. Even when I consider Braill a reaction to me and my meddling, he is emotionally unacceptable.

The unattractive picture of Braill with a cruel self-satisfied smirk on his face vanished suddenly, leaving me in a vacuum. The lights in the Washington to London plane cabin were turned on and we were told we would be landing in forty-five minutes. I had done a full review in sequence, without repeating myself. It had taken all the London to Washington trip, my night in Washington and the Washington to London return journey. Washington was receding.

I was not looking forward to what lay ahead, the contact with Raji, then back to Brandt, back to Raji, excitement, elation everywhere then—the moment it all stopped—destructive self-examination and fear. I don't know how the Brandts of this world cope with it all—or does he? I am determined to have that conversation with Brandt, I must find out what he wants to tell me. Perhaps I can induce him to speak by discussing my feelings towards Maddoun Saddeh, by telling him that Saddeh always reminded me of my brother Raouf, how his mere existence, even after "resigning", had become a reproach to me. Yes, I'll use that to unlock Brandt's enigmatic look.

What would Maggie think of what I was doing now? She'd remind me of my monologues against Khomeini and I would find an excuse to justify Dr. Raji. Yes, Maggie, I've become a whore. I am punishing you by confirming it, by being a simple boy scout in a Mickey Mouse game, just like the rest of them. I'm not going to worry anymore. I'll become a cross of Brandt and Butcher. I've found the way out, a way out.

"Do you live in London, sir?"

"Yes, I have been a resident here for six years."

"I see you were born in Jerusalem. How long have you been an American citizen? We are entitled to ask."

The immigration officer couldn't have been a day over twenty-one. It took a lot to stop me from exploding. What business was it of his? If he only knew, the little jerk, how American I was, what I had done for America and what I was doing for America now.

They usually ask if I have anything to declare. This ass wanted to know about my connection with America. Something has gone wrong with the world. How dare he.

The passport was stamped, the luggage was collected and a taxi was waiting. South Audley Street was the same, though you expect places to be different after long trips, even when the trips take a short time. It was only half past ten in the morning so I fed the cat and went into a deep sleep until seven in the evening.

Oh the call of the endless chatter, the need for noise. I went to the pub, I drank and drank and drank until it closed. I moved two blocks to an after hours place called L'Escapade. It was full of a young crowd committed to fruity, colorful drinks, but I stayed with my vodka and soda. I could hardly hear the deafening noise around me. I was in a world removed, different from L'Escapade except for a Middle East type who had made a mysterious appearance at the pub and now seemed to be eyeing me with interest at L'Escapade. I kept seeing him dialing my telephone number and saying nothing. Was he responsible for the mysterious calls? No, no, I must be imagining things.

The legs were feeling unsteady. Time to go home. Out on the street and a taxi home. The driver was reluctant to take me but finally did. I had a hard time pronouncing South Audley. My alcoholic dislocation wasn't helped by the inexplicable appearance of the staring young Arab, the mustachioed, black-eyed, slightly overweight son of a bitch of a would-be Iraqi, or PLO assassin working for the Iraqis. I just knew too much. Yes, I seemed to remember he had made another appearance at the pub a few days before my first visit to Anna. Then he did nothing except look at me. Perhaps he was a Shia Arab working for the Iranians or a hired hand of Brandt and Darrells. Yes, perhaps with the branch of the CIA which was paying the Palestinians blood money to protect the planes of All American Airways.

When the driver got me home the momentary sobriety of identifying a would-be killer had evaporated, and I had a bad time peeling off three pounds to pay him. The key wouldn't fit the lock for a long while. Everything was a bit more difficult. As a matter of fact, everything was whirling around. I spread my arms out to touch both sides of the hall to steady myself. I made it to the first floor with difficulty, but couldn't make it to the second floor except on all fours. I barely saw the figure of Ecstasy watching me from the top of the stairs, waiting for me to reach her.

I thought the painful crawl was over when I reached the top of the stairs. It wasn't. I crawled to the bedroom on all fours, grabbed the edge of the bed and climbed on top. I rolled over and closed my eyes to avoid the turning ceiling, to avoid thinking about where I was. Ecstasy jumped next to me and I made a half-hearted attempt to pet her. I foggily dismissed Darrells, Brandt and my pursuer and concentrated on what lay ahead, but Maggie and Blacks kept appearing. I tried to speak to Ecstasy. "Mummy's been gone for a while now. Mummy is all gone and sister Blacks is gone." And then I disappeared into a deep alcoholic sleep.

The telephone rang at seven thirty in the morning and I eventually managed to pick up the receiver ready to say hello and hear the other side's click. It wasn't so. My hello was answered by the intermittent clinging usually made by a pay telephone. The special effects noise stopped and the line cleared.

"Daoud, it's Raouf. I am sure I woke you up, I am sorry."

God it was lovely to hear his voice again, to hear love on the line again. "It's okay, it's okay. Where are you calling from? Father told me they haven't heard from you in six months."

"I'm in London, but please don't tell anyone—not a word."

"Of course not. You still don't trust anything except pay phones!" And the sound of brotherly laughter rang on both ends of the line.

"Yes . . . listen, can you meet me for a drink tonight?"

"Why not—that's all I do."

"Okay, do you know a place called Will Wentley's on Beauchamp Place—it's a wine bar?"

"Yes, know it well."

"Meet me there at six o'clock, exactly, and we'll talk."

"Exactly six."

"Yes, yes."

My head ached heavily. I reached for the glass of water next to the bed, took a big gulp and pulled the duvet over my head. My condition was worse than usual, cold sweat and an all-over body ache. I felt like an abused piece of machinery and I went back to sleep without difficulty to wake up at 2:30 p.m.

This time when the telephone rang I was writing a lengthy note to Anna, instructions for her to call the police about the bugged telephone and abbreviated notes on all that had happened including who to contact at some newspapers about the whole story. I told her that I would be in touch, but advised her against contacting me.

"Daoud, Jerry Dnipe, how are you?"

"I'm fine Jerry, saw your colleague in Washington. You are the man I want to hear from. As a matter of fact, it should be right away—any chance before six?"

"Sure, I'm at the Britannia Hotel."

"Great, that's less than a block away. Can I rush over in half an hour?"

"Sure. Are you alright?"

"Oh—yes, yes, but must see you."

A mad rush to shower and shave. The whole Dnipe thing was a godsend. He blew the cover off the CIA misdoings in Vietnam, published a book about it and lost a long, costly, painful legal case which forbids him to write anything about the Agency anymore. Jerry would tell me what to do, how to blow the whistle without suffering too much. I'm sure he knows a civil liberties group or someone else who could help. Yes Maggie, just watch and see, I'll show the bastards, I'll show them. I'm going to make so much noise it will reverberate to the heart of Wiltshire. Wait and see.

REPORT TO THE COMMAND OF THE POPULAR FRONT FOR THE LIBERATION OF PALESTINE

SUBJECT DAOUD AL MOUSA LEFT HIS RESIDENCE ON SOUTH AUDLEY STREET AT 3:00P.M. 7TH AUGUST 1983 FOLLOWED BY COMRADE ABU AL AIN. HE STOPPED AT A NEWSSTAND, BOUGHT SOME NEWSPAPERS AND CIGARETTES AND WENT INTO THE BRITANNIA HOTEL.

COMRADE ABU AL AIN REPORTS SUBJECT MET WITH AN AMERICAN MAN WHO IS OBVIOUSLY KNOWN TO HIM FOR TWO AND A HALF HOURS IN THE COFFEE SHOP OF THE HOTEL. THEY DRANK COFFEE AND PERRIER AND SPOKE IN HUSHED TONES, SUBJECT TALKING IN AN ANIMATED MANNER. THE AMERICAN MADE A FEW NOTES ON A PIECE OF PAPER HE PULLED OUT OF HIS POCKET.

SUBJECT LEFT HOTEL AT 5:45P.M., HAILED A CAB AT CORNER OF NORTH AUDLEY AND OXFORD STREETS. PER INSTRUCTIONS COMRADE ABU AL AIN DID NOT PURSUE HIM.

COMRADE ABU AL HUB, LOCATED AT TRATTORIA RESTAURANT IN BEAUCHAMP PLACE, REPORTED BY TELEPHONE THAT SUBJECT ARRIVED ACROSS THE STREET AT WILL WENTLEY'S WINE BAR AT 5:55P.M.

I TELEPHONED THE SUBJECT DAOUD AL MOUSA AT WILL WENTLEY'S WINE BAR AT EXACTLY 6:00P.M. A FEMALE VOICE ANSWERED AND I COULD HEAR THAT HE WAS BEING PAGED. I INSTRUCTED SUBJECT TO LEAVE THE WINE BAR IMMEDIATELY, TURN RIGHT, RIGHT AGAIN AND THEN TAKE THE SECOND LEFT, A DIMLY LIT SECLUDED COBBLESTONE ROAD LEADING TO A RESTAURANT CALLED DODOS. SUBJECT SAID HE WOULD, WITH IRRITATION.

THREE MINUTES AFTER, I COULD SEE SUBJECT TURN INTO COBBLESTONE ROAD WEARING A TRENCH COAT. AS I WAS HIDING BEHIND A TELEPHONE BOOTH, HE COULD NOT SEE ME AND MOVED FORWARD SLOWLY, LOOKING APPREHENSIVE.

WHEN I APPEARED FROM BEHIND THE TELEPHONE BOOTH THE SUBJECT MADE QUICK STEPS TOWARDS ME AND THEN STOPPED AND SMILED. SUBJECT ASKED "MAY I LEAVE A NOTE TO EITHER MARGIE OR MAGGIE?" IT WAS DIFFICULT TO TELL THE EXACT NAME BECAUSE OF THE BACKGROUND TRAFFIC NOISE. REQUEST WAS DENIED.

TRAITOR WAS ELIMINATED BY ME AT 6:05P.M. USING THE USUAL METHOD. HE MANIFESTED NO DESIRE TO FLEE AND OFFERED NO RESISTANCE. AS TRAITOR OPERATED ALONE, WE RECOMMEND THAT HIS FILE BE CLOSED.

LONG LIVE THE REVOLUTION.
COMRADE RAOUF AL MOUSA